MY
Hood King
GAVE ME A
LOVE LIKE NO
Other

A NOVEL BY

MISS JENESEQUA

BY MISS JENESEQUA

#TheFreakInTheBooks

SYNOPSIS

They've secretly been in love with each other from their very first encounter but convinced themselves that they mean nothing to one another, until one unexpected night, four days before her wedding to another man changes everything...

Indira Porter has always been a survivor. After a tragic event sets her whole life in a completely new direction, the only person she knows she can trust is herself—and Javon, her boyfriend. The pair are in love or... so it seems. In her mind, their love is real and secure enough to withstand the hardships of life. With their wedding just days away, Indira convinces herself that marrying Javon is the best thing to do, despite his imperfections. However, Indira's about to learn a big lesson. The difference between a boy who exploits her and a man who truly cherishes her.

Bakari Marshall: a man that many love and many love to hate. His attractive looks, irresistible smile, and intelligence doesn't take away from the ruthless, dominant individual he is. Being the only son of his parents meant that Bakari had to step up and be the protector of his entire family: his mother, father, and two crazy ass sisters who he would die for in a heartbeat. Grinding his way to the top meant that he could become the respected, feared, and envied man he is today. Falling in love was never part of his game plan, and if he did fall in love, he certainly didn't expect it to be with a beauty such as Indira. Someone that he believed was just a childhood acquaintance and someone who didn't care for his existence.

Indira's been acquainted to the quiet, humble, and no-nonsense side of Mr. Marshall before, but she's about to become well acquainted with the private, unusual side of him. The side that takes her to indescribable euphoria. The romance between Bakari and Indira consumes them both, becoming intense and too passionate for either party to resist. Despite all the odds saying they can't be together, Bakari makes it clear to Indira that she alone is who he wants. And the word 'no' just happens to not be in his vocabulary.

Can Indira allow herself to be with the one man that she's convinced herself for so long is just a product of her past? Or will her loyalty to her so-called fiancé stop her from beginning a new chapter with an infamous yet charming hood king? With secrets lurking in every corner... will Indira be able to trust herself or even anyone at all? In *My Hood King Gave Me A Love Like No Other*... love will certainly endure, but who is strong enough to win the war?

"Girls need love... girls need loving too
Girls need love too
So what's a girl to do when she needs loving too?"
Summer Walker♫

Chapter One

"So the audacity, the nerve of this nigga to tell me, 'Nah, girl, I don't eat pussy.'"

"And what did you say?"

"I said, 'That's crazy... but guess what? I don't eat pussy spelled backwards is I bet your bro will though.' Acting as if I won't cut his ass off and let his bro get all of this. Like I won't put this pussy on his brother."

Indira immediately began to giggle softly at the words her current client had revealed. Giggling too much wasn't on her agenda because she didn't want to lose focus on her task at hand. But having a funny client was something that could not be controlled, especially when that client happened to be the person signing off on her pay checks, her long-time childhood friend and boss, Tokyo Marshall.

"I ain't even a big sucker for head, but what you *not* about to do is act cocky and shit, acting as if eating pussy is a bad thing, but me sucking you off is a mandatory thing. Nah nigga, you and your ugly ass dick can get the fuck outta here."

Indira kept her lips tightly pressed together in an attempt to contain her laughter. She gently moved her tweezers across to the half-empty tray of individual mink lashes and picked one up. Then carefully using her other tweezer to separate Tokyo's lashes, she slowly inserted the lash into the last available gap on her lash line.

"Matter fact, I haven't gotten any dick in a long time. I can't tell whether my pussy's wet or she's crying," Tokyo said sulkily.

The laugh that Indira had tried so hard to conceal immediately came bursting out, and she had to lean up away from Tokyo so she wouldn't be laughing hysterically in her face.

"Girl, it's the truth," Tokyo admitted with a soft chuckle.

Indira let out her final laughs before leaning back down to apply the final touches on her work. She reached to the white gloss side table beside her for an eyelash comb and brush. The lash comb was slowly placed through Tokyo's lashes, straightening them out and making them look neater, then followed up with the mini brush to give the lash extensions that final perfect touch.

"All done, boss lady," Indira announced once lifting the brush off Tokyo's lashes.

Tokyo's eyes fluttered open, and she blinked rapidly for her watery eyes to adjust to the natural lighting of the room. As she sat up from the white beauty chair, she looked at the matching white walls before turning behind her to look at Indira. In Indira's hand was a silver heart-shaped mirror which she happily handed to Tokyo, making Tokyo smile with delight the moment she took it.

"These look so bomb," Tokyo complimented her as she admired her reflection. "You always know how to slay my lashes so damn well!"

"That's what I'm here for," Indira responded with a smile, watching her boss.

"That's why you're the best, Indi. I swear hiring you six months ago was the greatest idea. You have this place packed every single day with clients."

And that was the honest truth.

Eyelash extensions had been a hobby that Indira had started at age nineteen. She mostly did them on herself and her friends, and before she knew it, she had customers knocking on her door every day. What had started off as a hobby and something to keep her occupied when she wasn't in high school, quickly turned into a side hustle. A side hustle that paid extremely well. Now at the age of twenty-four, she had gotten her associate's degree and license in cosmetology from beauty school, got an additional license as an eyelash technician, and was now working full time in Tokyo Marshall's beauty salon.

Tokyo Marshall was the CEO of Tokyo's Slay Spot located in Castleberry Hill, downtown Atlanta. It was a beauty salon that did nails, hair, and eyelash extensions. But in addition to having a section for ladies, Tokyo had recently hired female barbers to cut hair.

Tokyo Marshall was known for two things: being crazy and being captivating. Her beauty was undoubtable. She was light skinned with large, round, mahogany eyes that drew you in from the very first glance. Her perfectly arched eyebrows framed her glowing, oval face. Her skin was blemish free with not a single flaw in sight. Being the owner of a beauty salon meant that Tokyo Marshall took pride in having flawless skin. Regular trips to her dermatologist was a must. Her brown hair was usually kept simple and left jet straight to flow around her. But this month, she had decided to dye it honey blonde, and today it was up in two buns. Tokyo stood at five feet two, petite, but not the one to mess with. Her body was cute too. She was slim but had a curvy frame.

Doing her boss's lashes after work hours was something that Indira was more than willing to do. Tokyo was a great boss who not only paid her well but gave her regularly, healthy bonuses. The large, monthly revenue that Indira brought to the salon from her lash extension clients meant that Tokyo was over the moon to give her bonuses.

And besides, with how booked and busy Indira was, the only way she could get Tokyo done was by doing her lashes after working hours. What Indira loved about her job was the fact that she had her own room set up in the shop. Most of the beauticians worked out front doing hair and nails, but only Indira had her own eyelash work space.

"You want a ride home, Indi?" Tokyo curiously asked as she got up from the recliner.

"I'm okay. Thanks," Indira respectfully declined, not wanting to bother her boss.

Tokyo placed her hands on her hips and gave Indira a skeptical look. She knew Indira couldn't drive, and she also knew that no one was coming to pick Indira up except for maybe an Uber.

"It's no longer a question, girl," Tokyo voiced coolly. "Get your shit and let's bounce. Come on. We gotta get you home to your fiancé."

A wide grin grew on Indira's lips at Tokyo's mention of her fiancé, Javon Thomas. They were getting married in seven days. Seven days that Indira badly wanted to rush through because spending the rest of her life with Javon as his wife was something that she desperately wanted to get started on.

Four years ago, Indira had lost her brother, Kieran, in a car crash. A car crash that had been caused by a drunk driver who had stupidly decided to get behind the wheel instead of taking a cab home. Indira felt like she had absolutely no one to turn to. Her father she rarely spoke to nowadays, and Kieran wasn't even his son, so he didn't share the same grief as Indira. As for her mother, she and Kieran weren't the closest pair, so even though that was her son that she had lost, Indira knew her mother wasn't as cut up about Kieran's death like she was.

The only person who Indira could turn to was Javon. He had shared a similar grief when losing his sister to a stray bullet in Chicago, where he was originally raised. Javon showed her a solace like no other and provided her with the love that she truly needed. Four years later, and she hadn't looked back since. They'd had their ups and downs but came out on top every time. So when Javon popped the question a year ago, the only option Indira could see was yes.

Fifteen minutes later, Indira thanked Tokyo for dropping her home, said her goodbyes, and left her red BMW i8. One thing about Tokyo was her love for sports cars, and she knew she got crazy stares all the time from bystanders in the streets of Atlanta. A tiny ass woman such as herself in a tiny yet luxurious, bright red sports car was bound to get looks. But that was exactly what she liked. A crazy red sports car to match her crazy self.

Indira and Javon lived in a one-bedroom apartment in the heart of Oakland City, a neighborhood located in Southwestern Atlanta. It wasn't one of the greatest neighborhoods, but for Indira, it had become home, and she had grown accustomed to it.

"Baby!" Indira yelled as she stepped into her home with her key in the door. "I'm home."

Her eyes scanned the living room and its four ivory walls as she shut the oak door behind her.

"Baby?"

Indira called out again to him as she dropped her work bag on a couch and began walking through their home. Her assumption had been that since she had arrived home slightly later than usual, Javon would already be home from work. However, after exploring through their home and seeing him nowhere in sight, Indira knew her assumption had been wrong.

A soft sigh seeped past her lips as she sat on the edge of her bed. Just as she rested her head back to lie down and get her mind right, the opening of the front door sounded, making her jump up and race excitedly to greet her fiancé.

"Javon, baby I thou..." Her words quickly trailed off when she arrived in the doorway of the living room. Seeing the sadness that clouded his features made her heart fill with concern, and she slowly began walking up to him.

"Baby, what's wrong?"

Javon Thomas was attractive. His attractive looks had been one of the reasons why she found him irresistible. He was only five eleven, but Indira was five eight, making him still taller than her, so she didn't mind. Also, since he had a slim physique, it made him appear even taller. His dark chocolate skin was the clearest, and it lowkey made her jealous at how clear his skin was without him spending hours on a skincare routine. On his head were dark brown dreadlocks that he liked to keep tied away from his face. He had plump, pink lips that Indira loved to suck on.

Javon was yet to respond to her query, making her even more worried. His brown eyes glistened as he watched her, and when Indira reached up to hold his warm face, the first tear dropped.

"Baby, talk to me," Indira pleaded as she pecked his lips and used her fingers to wipe away his tears. "Please."

A deep sigh left Javon's lips, and he shut his eyes in the hopes that the tears would stop falling.

"I... I got fired."

Hearing him reveal his news made a weight settle on her heart. *Again?* This was the fifth time this year that Javon had been fired from a job. He claimed that it wasn't him and that it was just the jobs that no longer wanted him. One time he said a job was having financial setbacks, and since he was the last employee hired, they were letting him go. Another time it was because they just no longer needed him, and another time, it had been because someone had returned to a company to get the job that he now had. Indira wondered what the reason would be this time.

"They said my hair was inappropriate," Javon revealed through gritted teeth as he opened his eyes. "My fucking hair."

"I don't believe this shit," Indira commented with dismay. "Fuck their racist asses. Can't you sue for wrongful termination?"

Javon immediately shook his head no. "Ain't no point. They'll have a good ass lawyer... a good ass lawyer that I can't afford, and before you say it, the answer is no, Indi. I don't want you wasting your hard-earned money on my shit."

"Your shit is my shit," Indira told him with a small smile, hoping to cheer him up. "Your problems are my problems."

He shook his head once again. "We're getting married in seven days. That's our shit that I want us focused on," he said before reaching for her left hand and lifting it off his face. "I can't wait to marry you." Then he looked down at her ring. A simple white gold engagement ring, the only thing he could afford in the shop at the time he was shopping around for rings.

"I promise you that I'll buy you a bigger ring once I get a ne—"

"Von, you don't need to—"

"I want to," he affirmed, cutting her off and giving her a serious stare. "I want to."

He kissed the top of her ring and then leaned down toward her so he could plant a gentle kiss on her soft lips. Their lips meshed together momentarily, and just as Indira parted her lips to welcome his tongue, Javon pulled their lips apart.

"You deserve to be treated, especially with how I keep making you pick up the rent."

Indira gave him a warm smile before responding, "It's nothing, babe. I got us. Always."

Javon returned her smile before placing his lips back on hers and giving her a taste of exactly what she craved.

While their lips collided, all Indira found herself doing was hoping and praying that Javon found a permanent job after their wedding and four-day honeymoon in Paris. Splashing out on an expensive honeymoon was something that Javon had voted against because he didn't want her paying for practically it all. So Indira agreed and let him talk her into waiting until he got a steady paying job so they could go on a glamorous honeymoon.

However, their honeymoon wasn't what Indira was worried about. They needed a new home to start the next chapter of their married lives, but how could they do that if Indira was the only one bringing in money?

"You spray painted my car? Really, Tokyo? You stupid, little bitch. You know how much that shit's gonna cost me? You used multiple spray paints!"

"Watch your mouth, homie," Tokyo retorted, keeping her eyes on the road ahead. "You know who my brother is? And you know he shoots dudes like you for fun. So watch that mothafuckin' mouth before I give you something to cry like a stupid, little bitch about." She then chuckled as she remembered what she had done to an old fling's car last night. It was a brand-new whip too, so she was more than happy to spray paint it. "You wanted to be slick and talk to other girls while messing with me, so I showed you some slick shit by giving your car a new paint job. Enjoy, love."

"Tokyo, I swear you will pay for th—"

"Don't hit my line again, Carl," Tokyo said before pressing the end call button on her car phone screen.

I really need to be celibate, Tokyo mused as she continued driving her car along the freeway. Messing around with guys just didn't seem to be fun anymore. They were either already in a relationship or just looking to have sex. And most of the time, Tokyo was down for the sex, but she craved more. She craved having someone to text all day when they were apart and someone to come home to. Someone to kiss and cuddle with all night. But all of that seemed very unlikely with all the men she kept on entertaining. *No more of this bullshit. I'm done with men from here on out.* She would stay focused on her business and her coins, the two main things that made her happy in this life.

Chapter Two

Another day, another dollar.

Indira had been fully booked all day. She was even busier than usual because she had put up an Instagram post and Facebook post on her business social media accounts, last Friday, that she would be off duty in a few days. From that day onwards, she had been getting an overload of emails, comments, and direct messages. Women had been begging to get an appointment with her, but she couldn't say yes to everybody.

Right now, she had just finished up a client's lashes and was going to head out on her lunch break. What she craved was some seafood boil from *Bon Ton Atlanta* which was thirteen minutes by car. An Uber would get her there in no time.

Indira knew how bad it was that she couldn't drive a car, but with how busy she was with work all the time, learning how to drive was the last thing on her mind. Sooner or later, she would make it a priority. Hopefully.

Indira grabbed her phone that was sitting on her work desk, about to request her Uber, when she remembered how much Tokyo loved seafood boil. So she got up from her seat and walked out her work space to head to Tokyo's office next door. The comfortability that

Tokyo allowed her to feel made Indira gently push open the closed door and knock while walking in.

"Boss lady, I'm he..." She immediately wished this time she had knocked. "I'm so sorry," Indira quickly announced.

Her eyes were on Tokyo's momentarily before they landed on the mesmerizing eyes of the man who had just turned to face her. The man that strangely made her heart flutter without saying a single word.

"No, don't be, Indi!" Tokyo exclaimed, raising her hand to greet her. "My brother just came to annoy me for the day."

Indira gave her a shy smile before looking back over at him as he stood by the window blinds.

"Hi, Bakari."

When God created this man right here, he knew exactly what he was doing. Exactly what he was doing. He had created an extremely good-looking man. Standing at six feet five, Bakari Marshall took over any room that he was in. The dark gray short sleeved shirt he was wearing revealed his large muscular arms, and just from the way his shirt perfectly covered his body, Indira could tell that hiding under-neath was the body of a Greek god. In addition to his gray short sleeved shirt, he also wore black Balmain jeans and all black Nike Air Max 270's on his feet. Peeking under his shirt was a simple silver chain, a matching silver stud locked in each ear, and on his wrist was a silver iced out Rolex watch that almost blinded Indira from the moment she stared at it. He wasn't the super flashy type, but he still looked good and paid nonetheless.

Bakari had honey golden skin that was smooth and even. His face was chiseled and housed a moustache on the edge of his pink, full, juicy looking lips that extended into a healthy low-cut beard. On his head were 360-degree waves so deep and wavy that you could drown in them. He had the sharpest line up and two slits in his hair. His thick brows suited his face well. But those eyes? Those deep-set eyes were the real problem. They were cocoa brown with specks of light brown. And they never failed to capture one's attention. He said nothing in return to her but greeted her with a friendly smile, revealing his gleaming white teeth.

"What's up, Indi? You sounded like you had something important to say," Tokyo voiced while staring at her carefully.

Indira broke eye contact with him and looked back at Tokyo. "Oh yeah. I just wanted to know if you wanted anything from Bon Ton? I'm heading there now to grab some lunch."

"Oh my gosh! For sure! That's so funny because I've been craving it all damn day."

While his sister told Indira exactly what she wanted for lunch, Bakari stood stoically by the blinds, carefully observing Indira. *I ain't seen her pretty ass in months...* And it was true. Bakari hadn't seen Indira since the day she started working for his sister. Coming around to Tokyo's salon was rare, and even though he had invested into her business, Bakari preferred his sister doing what she did best and having full control. He had simply given her the remaining funds that she had needed to start her shit up.

Finding out that Tokyo was hiring Indira wasn't a big shock but a shock nonetheless. He hadn't laid eyes on her in years. Even though they lived in the same city, they didn't run in the same circles. The only reason why they knew each other in the first place was because of Indira and Tokyo's friendship. They had gone to high school together, and whenever Bakari would come to pick Tokyo up, he would always offer Indira a ride home. An offer that she always declined.

Indira Porter.

She seemed to have only gotten finer with time. Like him, she was light skinned and had the most delicate looking skin. Skin that made him want to rub her down all night with jojoba oil. Her jet-black hair was bone straight, in a middle parting, and fell past her waist. She had the softest, most luscious looking pink lips that were glossy and plump. And her chestnut eyes told the sweetest story without her saying a word. Time had also done her body well. Very well indeed. What used to be a skinny, bony five-foot-eight frame was now filled out well with curves, thick thighs, a well-rounded butt, and medium sized breasts. And of course her eyelashes were long and full, courtesy of her own skills. Beautiful was an understatement to describe Ms. Porter.

When Tokyo had finished telling Indira what she wanted, Indira said her goodbyes and took her leave.

"T, I ain't about to tell you again," Bakari sternly warned Tokyo. "Ou menm ak Arjana bezwen pale *(You and Arjana need to talk)*."

Indira caught the sound of his voice as she left Tokyo's office, resulting in her heart to flutter once again. Even his voice was a problem. He had the deepest, smoothest voice that settled within her core and made her feel like her insides were melting. And to hear him speak his native Haitian Creole tongue so sexily was something that made her cheeks hot.

"Fuck her," Tokyo snapped, reaching across her desk for her phone. "She ain't even my real sister."

Not hearing his response made Tokyo look up from her bright screen only to quickly regret it. He was giving her a nasty glare, a glare that told her one thing.

"Alrighttttt," she lightly sang. "I take that back. She is my real sister, but what am I supposed to do? Kari, li te kòmanse sou mwen! *(Kari, she started on me!)*"

Arjana Marshall was their half-sister. They shared the same mother but not the same father. Bakari and Tokyo's father was Haitian, and their mother African-American, whereas Arjana had a Filipino father. Arjana had been the product of their mother's first relationship which hadn't ended well at all. Arjana's father was now in jail for murdering a man, and Arjana never spoke to him. So in reality, the only family she had was their mother and them. That's why Bakari made it his duty to lookout for her and Tokyo. It was only the three of them, and they had to stick together no matter what.

"I don't care who started on who," Bakari snapped. "You need to fix things, period."

Tokyo sighed with annoyance at his order. As much as she wasn't trying to talk to her older sister after their nasty argument, she knew that with Bakari now getting involved, she had no choice. He never got involved in their domestics, so for him to be getting involved now meant that shit was serious.

"Fine," she agreed with a defeated look. "But if she starts on me again, I swear, Kari, I won't talk to her ever again."

Bakari walked away from the blinds, ready to take his leave.

"You can make shit right today by calling her," he informed her coolly, giving her one last glance before turning toward the door.

"Calling her? Hell no, I ain't calling he..."

Tokyo's words trailed off when Bakari stopped in his stance and slowly turned back to her. The look on his face was neutral, but Tokyo knew her brother better than she knew herself. It would be neutral for just a few seconds, but as soon as she spoke up, it would switch into a look she didn't want to see.

"What was that?"

Tokyo rolled her eyes at her brother, knowing that if she repeated what she had previously said, he would most definitely snap on her once again.

"Calling her is fine, Kari. I'll do it tonight," she announced with a fake smile.

Bakari gave her a satisfied head nod before reaching for the golden handle and taking his leave. His plan had been to go through the salon, but then he remembered how much of a scene it was whenever he walked through. Tokyo's workers and their clients were always gassed over seeing him. A few had the balls to actually say hi and a few too shy but always giving him lustful looks. So he took the back exit before heading to his black Aston Martin parked in the back parking lot of Tokyo's salon.

As Bakari drove through the streets of Atlanta, there was only one person on his mind. *Damn, where the hell she been?* Seeing Indira again after so long evoked feelings of nostalgia in him. He didn't know why, but from the very first day he had laid eyes on her, he had the sudden urge to embrace her and keep her safe, promising to never let any harm come to her. And alongside that urge, he had another urge to kiss h—

Bakari's thoughts were disrupted by his car's touchscreen unit that was now notifying him of an incoming call. He tapped the answer button and waited for the caller to talk.

"Yo, B."

It was Yasir Halim.

Bakari wasn't one to have too many friends. He kept his circle small and trusted no one really but himself. However, if he had to say who his best friend was in this life, it would be Yasir, no doubt. Yasir was someone who he had known for years now, and they worked well together. But having a best friend wasn't something he truly believed in.

"Yasir," Bakari greeted him simply.

"Found him," Yasir said. "The nigga that stole the keys of coke? He's at Connie's dow—"

Bakari didn't even wait for Yasir to finish his sentence. He ended the call and immediately began racing to the next available exit. Adrenaline and rage filled his veins. Every muscle in his body tensed up as he drove to Connie's. Any prior positive thoughts or feelings he had been having were all gone. The only thing he wanted now was bloodshed.

He arrived at Connie's ten minutes later, pulling up and parking right outside. As he got out of his car, he was greeted to Yasir who had a smirk on his face.

"He's seated at the back of the diner," Yasir told him as he lifted a dap to Bakari. "Connie knows what's up."

Bakari quickly lifted his fist to return the dap before pulling open the front entrance and entering the diner.

The smell of fried chicken, burgers, and French fries immediately filled his nostrils. He took long, bold strides into the diner, staring stoically at the few customers sitting in booths.

Connie, the owner of the diner, stood by the bar, and upon seeing Bakari, a smile graced her red lips, and she gave him a sexy wink before nodding toward the back of the restaurant.

Luke had been too occupied getting stuck in his meal to fully notice the two men that had entered the diner, and who were now walking into the diner. But when his eyes finally looked up, he was barely able to breathe.

"Now would you look at that?" Yasir spoke up proudly while Bakari pulled out the empty chair in front of Luke. "The one man we've been looking for everywhere."

Staring into the eyes of Bakari Marshall made Luke's stomach turn. The way his eyes currently bore into him had him wanting to be swallowed by the ground right this instant.

"I-I-I-I I've been away."

"Away?" Bakari finally spoke up with a curious look as he leaned back in his chair.

"Y-Yes," Luke nervously stated, silently coaching himself to get it together. "My mom's been sick, so I've been looking after her."

"Hear that, Yasir?" Bakari looked up at Yasir who was standing beside him. "His mother's been sick."

"Sick? Well that ain't no good."

"No good at all," Bakari said sympathetically before locking eyes with Luke once again. "How long she been sick for?"

"...A few weeks now," Luke responded after swallowing hard.

"Damn," Bakari remarked with a head shake. "That's crazy. Ain't that crazy, Yasir?"

"Some real crazy shit," Yasir replied with a frown.

"Some real crazy shit," Bakari repeated after him, finessing his fingers through his beard. "You wanna know why that's some crazy shit, Luke?"

Luke gave him a look of wonder, relief starting to fill his insides at the thought of Bakari believing him.

"I said, you wanna know why that's some crazy shit, Luke?" Bakari repeated, his voice laced with impatience.

"Why, boss?" Luke quickly asked, knowing that Bakari wasn't one to not be answered to.

"'Cause a few weeks ago, a friend hit me up, telling me an address," Bakari explained coolly. "You know what address I'm talkin' about?"

"No, boss."

"You sure about that?"

"Yes," Luke replied, genuinely feeling confused by the turn the conversation had taken.

"A friend hit me up telling me the address of where your mother is buried."

Luke's mouth instantly turned dry, and his chest tightened with fear. Bakari leaned forward in his seat, placing an elbow on the silver table and resting his chin on his fist while keeping his gaze on Luke. Then a smirk grew on his lips as he cocked his head to the side.

"You got another living mother I don't know about, Luke?"

Luke slowly shook his head no, unable to have the guts to actually speak up.

"Do you?"

"N-N-No, boss."

"So why the fuck did you just lie to me?" Bakari refused to break eye contact with him, and the fact that he had yet to blink had Luke on edge. "Huh?"

"I-I-I don't kn—"

A hollow, cold chuckle suddenly sounded out of Bakari's lips, making Luke's legs underneath the table shake. Even his hands that were no longer holding onto their cutlery were now shaking.

"I'ma tell you what I do know though," Bakari announced. "I know you enjoyed that meal very well, which is good considering that it's your last."

Luke's eyes widened with shock, and before he could respond, Bakari reached across the table for his fork while getting up from his seat. Before Luke could even realize what was about to happen, Yasir had moved closer to Luke, grabbed his neck, and forced his head up. Luke didn't even have the chance to scream out for help because Yasir placed a hand over his mouth, muffling his cries. Luke felt Yasir's arm choke his head up, and with his free hand, Yasir forced Luke's left eye open, allowing Bakari to jam the silver fork straight into Luke's eye.

It was an agony that Luke hadn't been prepared for. But what he definitely hadn't been prepared for was Yasir pushing the fork deeper into his eye. Then he dragged him out of his seat and took him through the back doors of the restaurant. At this point, he could only see through one eye, but even his one good eye left was blurry and struggling to cope with being his only source of vision. So Luke was unable to properly see where he was being led, but when he felt his body being pushed into a space, he tried to run away, only to collide into a wall and fall smack down on the concrete ground.

"Stupid nigga," Yasir commented with a light laugh at Luke's silly escape attempt. "Ain't no running today. You not only steal from B, but you lie to him too? Nah, you were asking to die, boy."

Bakari walked up to Luke, observing him carefully as he lay on the ground and groaned out in pain. The fork he had jammed into his eye was still there, and thanks to Yasir pushing it deeper, blood was gushing out his socket at an uncontrollable rate. None of that was Bakari's concern though. He lifted a foot to Luke's neck once near his body and gently pressed down on it with his shoe.

"Did you steal the keys, Luke?"

"...I... B-Bakari, p-please b—"

"Did you steal the keys, Luke?"

"...Ye—"

Bang!

"Ahhhhhh!" Luke's screams filled the room, but it didn't faze Bakari or Yasir one bit. Bakari hadn't shot him dead yet but simply shot him in his left arm.

"Guys are on their way," Yasir voiced once looking up from his phone.

"Cool," Bakari simply responded, ignoring Luke's wails.

Luke never got to finish confessing his crime. But he didn't have to. He had been caught on CCTV stealing product from Bakari's main dope spot, southwestern Atlanta.

"P-Please, Bakari! I'm s-sorry. Please! Don't kill me." Luke cried.

A large grin instantly formed on Bakari's lips as he stared down at Luke who was bleeding profusely.

"I'm not planning to kill you," Bakari announced as Luke felt hope rise within him. "Yet." Luke's hope instantly dropped. "I'm going to teach you a lesson about what happens when you steal from me. You used those hands to steal from me, so there's only one solution. With the one good eye you have left, you're going to watch your hands burn piece by piece. Then you're going to die."

"No, please, Bakar—"

"Shut the fuck up," Yasir snapped before hovering his boot above the fork still in Luke's eye, "before I push this shit so deep you'll feel it in your brain."

Thinking that you could steal from Bakari and get away with it was a big mistake. Being Haitian meant that he didn't play any games at all. Messing with him was basically you committing suicide. Luke was going to learn that fact the hard way before taking his last breath and joining his mother.

Chapter Three

"Bakari says I need to apologize to you, so I'm here to apologize."

"Well you and Bakari can follow three simple steps," Arjana said simply. "Take your apology, wrap it up, and stick it up both your asses."

Tokyo's face instantly scrunched up into a scowl as she looked at her sister. Out of the goodness of her heart, Tokyo had decided to go out of her way to visit her sister instead of giving her a simple phone call. However, instead of letting her inside her home, Arjana had Tokyo locked out on the other side of her screen door, watching her through it.

Tokyo continued to eye her sister with a nasty glare then decided to speak up. "Arjana, I came here to apologize, and you're still acting like a little brat," she snapped. "Which is funny considering you're supposed to be my older sister, but here I am being the mature one."

"You know damn well that if Bakari hadn't sent you to me, you would not be here right now," Arjana told her knowingly. "So stop trying to act like a little angel because you're not."

"So you're not going to accept my apology?"

Arjana kept her hands on her hips and said nothing in return to her sister. Their argument may have seemed silly, but to Arjana, it hurt to hear her sister tell her truths about herself. What had started off as a little back and forth quarrel due to Arjana finding out that Tokyo had taken her favorite dress without her permission, turned into Tokyo calling out Arjana for being a nobody and having nowhere to dress up for anyways.

Every woman in Atlanta who was somebody made sure they got their nails, hair, or eyelashes done at Tokyo's Slay Spot. It was the salon to be at, and even the *Real Housewives of Atlanta* shot a few episodes there for their reality TV show.

Tokyo had come up with the idea for her salon all by herself and made it into something big. She was a popular woman and successful all at the age of twenty-four. Knowing that she was twenty-seven and didn't have half of the success her younger sister had was something that made Arjana envious. It wasn't something she meant to feel, but seeing how well her sister was doing in life made Arjana feel like her life was nothing in comparison to Tokyo's. Sure she loved her younger sister with all her heart, but knowing that she didn't have her life mapped out the way Tokyo did was discouraging to say the least.

"Would you accept my apology if you were in my shoes, T?" Arjana questioned her with a suspicious look.

Tokyo bit the inside of her cheek, contemplating to herself for a while before responding, "At first, no... I wouldn't. But I would understand that you said things out of anger; things that you didn't mean."

Arjana softly sighed as she kept watching her sister through the screen. As hurt as she had been by Tokyo's words, she was more hurt by the fact that she didn't have her sister to call or text every day. She missed her company and their conversations.

Tokyo observed as Arjana stepped forward and slowly unlocked the screen door. Tokyo stepped back as she pushed it forward and was face to face in front of her without a boundary in between them anymore. Then Arjana stepped to the side, leaving a space for her younger sister to enter through, which she took with a happy grin on her face.

"Finalllyyy," Tokyo excitedly sang as she walked into the house. "You got a goon like me apologizing like a weak ass."

Arjana rolled her eyes, about to close the screen door, when she felt her body being hugged. She looked down to see Tokyo embracing her.

"I missed your mean ass though," Tokyo commented with a loving smile. "I'm sorry, Ana."

"I missed you too, T," Arjana responded, embracing her back. "Now get your lil' ass off me, woman."

Tokyo giggled lightly as she broke their embrace, took off her black leather jacket, hung it up on a coat rack, and hung her Gucci backpack.

"You cooked anything?" Tokyo queried as she left Arjana's front foyer and headed through her home to the kitchen. "I'm hungry."

"Lucky for you, I just finished making adobo and pancit."

Tokyo's mouth started watering up after hearing Arjana explain what she had made. And as soon as she got closer to the kitchen, the smell of freshly cooked chicken hit her nose buds. One thing that Tokyo loved about having a half-sister was her Filipino side that Arjana got from her father. So always having access to a Filipino cuisine courtesy of her sister was something that Tokyo truly cherished.

"You did what?"

"Gave his car a new paint job," Tokyo said nonchalantly before stuffing her mouth with more chicken. "What?"

Arjana's mouth was open wide, and her eyes were bulging as she looked at Tokyo. Then she burst into laughter, still in shock at her sister's antics.

"You crazy, lil' woman," she said.

"He's lucky I did a paint job and nothing else," Tokyo voiced after swallowing her food. "I could have put sand and water up in his gas tank and really fucked shit up. Matter fact, I might go do that too."

"T!" Arjana burst into more laughter. "Leave that man alone. You've already terrorized him enough."

"He's the real terrorizer," Tokyo answered. "Talking to other girls and shit after telling me he only wanted to be exclusive with me. How you got the next bitch calling me and asking who am I? Nigga, I'm your new worst nightmare, how about that? But it's cool. I'm done with men. I'm just going to be celibate for the rest of my life."

Arjana instantly released a scoff which made Tokyo give her a strange look.

"What?"

"Celibate my ass. The next dick that comes prancing into your life, you'll be all over that."

"Will not," Tokyo protested. "I'm done with dicks. All of them! It's time for Tokyo to do me."

"Alright, girl. If you say so."

"Speaking of dicks, how's yours?"

"Who?"

Tokyo smirked at her sister trying to act dumb.

"You know who."

"No clue who you're talking about," Arjana replied before adding, "I'm just keeping it strictly professionally between us from here on out. We work together, and that's it. Nothing else. He's focused on re-opening up the tattoo spot on Friday, and that's what I'm focused on too."

"You still trying to open up your own tattoo shop this year?"

Arjana nodded firmly.

"One hundred and ten percent. I'm just trying to save up a little bit more and get my clientele up."

"I could always chip i—"

"No, T." Arjana cut her off. "Bakari already tried, and I don't want you trying either. I appreciate you both so much, but I wanna do this on my own. I need to."

Tokyo gave her an understanding look before nodding. "A'ight, Mrs. Independent. I hear and feel you."

Arjana smiled lovingly at her sister and watched her finish the last remaining pieces of her meal.

Being a tattoo artist had always been Arjana's passion. She'd just never had the balls to pursue it until last year. Her dream was to open up her own tattoo shop, but she didn't want help from her brother or sister. She wanted to do this all by herself and that she planned to do. It was time to buckle up and make her dreams a reality. No more playing around.

- 2 Days Later -

"You're good with locking up the shop?" Tokyo asked gently as she stood in the doorway of Indira's work room.

"Yup," Indira said with a sure nod.

It was currently 6 p.m., and the store shut down in two hours. But Indira still had three clients left to do. And each set of individual mink eyelashes took two hours. But because Indira was skilled at her craft, she could do it in one hour and thirty minutes.

The salon closed at 8 p.m., but because Indira had an overload of clients on her last day, today she would be closing the shop up. She offered to do it because she didn't want Tokyo waiting around for her to finish. Closing up the salon wasn't an issue, and it wasn't like she hadn't done it before.

"Alrightie," Tokyo said with a smile. "Knock on my door if you need anything before I go."

"I will," Indira promised, returning a smile and watching as Tokyo left the doorway.

Her next client was running slightly late, so she patiently waited and made sure everything was in order for her next client.

Ding!

Indira looked over at her white side table to see her phone light up. She picked up her phone to examine the incoming text that had come in.

Bae, can I borrow a few dollars... as soon as I get my last check from this job I'll pay you back.

Javon.

Indira slowly typed back, *No problem love. I'll cash app you some money now. How much?*

Javon: *400.*

Indira frowned slightly at his requested amount. *How is that a few dollars?*

Indira: *Alrightie.*

Javon: *Have fun at your last day of work.*

Indira: *Thank you, baby.*

Javon: *I'll be home late tonight... Got some errands to run.*

Indira: *Errands?*

Javon: *Yeah bae. Errands.*

Javon: *I'll be back before you know it.*

Indira: *I'll be home late tonight too... I've got appointments till 10pm. Possibly later, depending on when I finish up.*

Javon: *10pm? Can't you leave earlier?*

Indira: *I can't abandon my clients, Von.*

Javon: *I'm not comfortable with you coming home so late.*

Indira stared down at his text message with a frown. He was the one that was running errands in the middle of the night, and she hadn't said anything about it. Her reason for coming home late was valid, but Javon was the one being demanding when his reason wasn't valid enough at all.

Javon: *But I know you gotta work so do your thing.*

Javon: *I love you and I'll see you later on tonight.*

Javon: *Don't forget about the money.*

Indira: *Okay.*

Javon borrowing money from her was nothing new. He practically did it all the time, and seeing as that was her man, she allowed him to. Whether he paid it back though, that was a rarity.

Their wedding was officially in four days. Surprisingly, Indira wasn't nervous. Her excitement levels changed constantly every day. One minute she was excited, then the next not so much. More so scared. Scared that she was getting married at the age of twenty-four. Was she too young to be in a marriage? Was she even ready for one? But instead of answering her questions, Indira blocked them out. Trying to make herself excited again at the thought of wearing her wedding dress and walking down the aisle.

Her wedding to Javon was a small one. Only her mother would be there, and her god sister, Emaza, was planning to fly into Atlanta in three days for the wedding. She didn't really have a lot of friends because her main focus had always been work. The only friend she had invited was Tokyo, who happily agreed to attend. Javon's father was coming, and his brother and best friend too. His mother had passed away when he was nine due to a spontaneous brain hemorrhage that doctors linked to her strong cocaine use. Javon was just grateful to have at least one parent still in his life and able to attend his wedding.

The wedding was a small one indeed, and seeing as Javon wasn't a religious person like her, she agreed with his suggestion of them having it in a courthouse. It wasn't what she wanted, but she didn't want to fuss about it. And she didn't want him unhappy. It was what it was.

Five minutes later, her client came rushing through the door and apologized for being late.

"It's alright, love," Indira stated affectionately. "Let's just get started."

Knowing that a hair which grew out from your eyelid not only protected your eye but accentuated your beauty had always fascinated Indira. Not having the longest lashes always made her feel disheartened... until she stumbled upon a YouTube tutorial that exposed her to the best next thing: eyelash extensions. And from that moment on, Indira hadn't looked back since.

- 4 hours and 30 minutes later -

Indira gently yawned as she stretched her arms up in the air. Her last client of the night was completed and had just walked out. Now all that was left for her to do was pack up her stuff and head home.

She wanted her warm bed more than anything in the world right now. Not even seeing Javon made her anxious to get home. All she wanted was some sleep.

Once tidying up her table and making the room tidy, Indira picked up her bag and began searching inside it for her ring. She had taken it off while working to keep her hands unoccupied, something that she always did every day.

However, the more she searched into her large H&M tote bag, the more dread started to fill her when she realized that her ring wasn't appearing to her.

Where the hell is i—

"Spray that shit!" someone suddenly yelled on the other side of the door, interrupting her thoughts. It was a male voice. "Ain't no camera about to stop me."

Her heart skipped a beat when she heard a crash followed by a bang and then a smash. More smashes followed, and it made her jump with fright at each one. They sounded violent and only made Indira fill with panic.

What the hell is going on? Indira mused as she quickly walked up to the door about to grab the handle and head outside only to realize how stupid that was. So instead of opening the door, she latched the door locked. *I can't go out there. They have weapons for sure... I need to call the police, right now.*

"Yeah, fuck all this shit up! I don't care! Ruining her shit just like she ruined mine," the male voice fumed. "You got the petrol, right? Start spreading that shit around cause we setting this bitch on fire tonight. Only thing I wanna see is flames. Burn it all right down to the ground!"

Indira almost collapsed at his words. *Get it together, Indi. Just call the police, and this will be over before you know it. They'll all be in jail by midnight.*

Indira decided to follow her own advice and whipped out her iPhone from her tote bag. She anxiously began pressing her home button to unlock her phone, but when the screen didn't pop up right away, she frowned. Pressing it a couple more times but having an undesired result made Indira's legs tremble. *No, no, no! Please God, no!*

Her phone was dead. However, that wasn't the main big issue. The main big issue was today had been the day that Indira had accidentally forgotten her charger which meant she had no way of charging her phone and... no way of contacting the cops.

"Ayo, put petrol in that separate work room and her office too. I want every single part of this salon burned to ashes. That'll teach her dumb ass not to spray paint my car. Crazy bitch."

Chapter Four

Indira's pulse was racing. Life had seemed so easy and calm less than ten minutes ago. Now here she was, stuck in the worst predicament of her life. Stuck in a situation that she had no clue about.

When Indira heard heavy footsteps walking toward the door, she instantly stepped back and looked down at the door handle while her eyes welled up. The golden doorknob began to twist repeatedly, but the door didn't open due to the latch that Indira had put in place. *Breathe, Indi. You're safe in here. There's no way he's getting in.*

"Ayo, Carl!" the male voice yelled out. "The door's locked."

"Well break that shit down then. Fuck wrong with you!" the male voice from the beginning shouted in response. "I want every last inch of this place up in flames."

"A'ight, bet!"

Her lips started to tremble, and she continued to step back until her back hit the white wall behind her. *I'm going to die today.* The tears that had formed in her eyes dropped once the first hit of the door sounded.

Bam!

Indira had not felt a fear like this in a long time. She couldn't even pinpoint the last time that she had felt this much fright. All she did was work Monday to Friday, so where was the time to be afraid?

Bam!

From the man on the other side of the door trying to knock down the door and the smashes she could hear coming from the salon, Indira's tears were constant. Her breathing was so fast, and she was trying to gulp down breaths to stay quiet so she wouldn't be heard.

Bam!

But what good would that do when the door was beginning to give way to his hits? He would be in soon and see Indira standing here with wet cheeks. But she was sure that it wouldn't faze him. Criminals didn't care about anyone but themselves. *I don't want to die. Not yet, God, please.*

Indira almost released a scream when she heard a hard kick. The intruder was no longer hitting against the door with his body but now delivering solid kicks to the side of the lock.

No longer wanting to see the door, Indira shut her eyes and clamped her hand over her mouth. She continued to silently pray, hoping that whatever happened through this situation, God would stay by her side. *Please God, pro—*

"Retreat! Retreat!" the male leader suddenly exclaimed which resulted in the kicks to stop. "We gotta get the fuck outta here! Now!"

"What's going o... Oh shit!"

Footsteps running through the salon were heard until they had run right through the back door. The lump that had formed in the back of Indira's throat quickly vanished, but that didn't stop her tears from flowing. She dropped to the floor against the wall, cradled her knees, and buried her face between her thighs. Her sobs were uncontrollable. A part of her was traumatized while the other part was extremely thankful to be alive.

She knew that if those men had gotten in, they would not let her live to tell the tale of tonight. The last faces she would have ever seen would have been theirs. Indira was relieved to know that they had gone. But why had they gone away? What exactly had drove them away? Or better yet, who?

Indira wanted to look up from her thighs, but she couldn't lift her head up. The trauma from the unexpected events were still within her. Even getting up now seemed like a tedious task. However, upon hearing footsteps walking toward the door, Indira's head slowly lifted up. She watched as the door handle turned once and then it was released once the person on the other side of the door realized it was locked.

"Indira, open the door."

Without even being able to stop it, her heart fluttered at the sound of his voice. Knowing that he was on the other side of the door right now and had basically come to save her, had Indira extremely grateful.

She managed to get up and saunter toward the door. When reaching it, she lifted her hand to the latch only to notice her shaky hands. Shock still settled within her from the prior events, but nonetheless, she plucked the courage to unlock the door.

The door was pulled open, and Bakari laid eyes on her pretty face. Seeing her puffy, tearful eyes and wet cheeks made the anger in his heart grow even more. Not liking the fact that he was able to see her so weak made her quickly wipe her tears away.

"B-Bakari," she croaked out, smiling weakly at him. But it was no use, because he could see right through her act, and she knew it too.

He was dressed in black from head to toe. An all-black Nike track-suit and black Nike Air Max 97's on his feet. His hoodie that had been up over his head, he pulled down. The color black suited him perfectly. He was the dark knight that had come to save her from the torment of criminals.

"Did they get in?"

His question was sharp and direct, and just from the way his jaw tightened and the serious look in his brown eyes, Indira knew he was pissed.

"No," she whispered, gazing up at him. "N-No... they... they didn't." The tears that she had wiped away were making an appearance again. And as Bakari watched a tear fall out her eye, his heart only broke further.

"T-They didn't," Indira repeated, thinking that by talking, she would stop herself from crying. "They didn't... g-get in." It was a useless, pointless thought because it didn't work. Her tears only fell quicker, and the water works wouldn't stop.

She took a step back into the room, about to turn away from him, until he stepped closer to her. He lifted a hand to her face and began to wipe away her tears. Indira stared up at him with shock as she felt him gently wipe away her tears. The look in his eyes as he watched her was a mixture of sadness and compassion.

Once her tears were wiped, Bakari stepped even closer toward her. His seductive cologne had already hit her nostrils from the minute she opened the door for him, but now it consumed her. It was a smell that she happily wanted to drown in.

She continued to look up at him, feeling slightly intimidated by how much he towered over her like a giant. When she felt his hands grab onto the sides of her waist before sliding across to cradle her back, Indira felt right at home. Instinctively, she placed the side of her head to rest on his chest, listening to his steady, strong heartbeat and lifting her arms to hold his body in return. This was a comfort that she needed, and since he was providing it, Indira would happily receive it.

Her and Bakari never talked... okay, *never* was an exaggeration, but for them to say more than 'hi' to one another was a rare thing. And most of the time, it was always her saying hi and he gave her smiles; nothing else, nothing more. But there was a reason that Bakari never uttered significant words to her. Ever since she had declined his offers of him dropping her home, years ago when Tokyo and she were in high school, Bakari just assumed that she did not like or care for him. So he left her alone and only spoke to her when she spoke to him.

Indira sighed softly when she felt his large hands rubbing on her back. His touch was putting her greatly at ease, and at this very moment, Indira felt ten times better than she had felt before. Then she heard his voice again, and butterflies flew in her stomach.

"Indira, that bullshit that happened tonight," he announced, "I swear on my life that that shit won't happen ever again. I won't ever let anyone hurt you."

His words were so assuring, which was strange, because she didn't even know him well enough. But she trusted him, and being in his arms only made her trust him wholeheartedly. She didn't even speak up to ask him how he knew to come to the salon and how he had figured out what was going. But again, she trusted him wholeheartedly. In his arms, she felt protected and loved. And most of all, she felt appreciated.

Indira lifted her head up and gazed into his chestnut irises. Her knees started to feel weak when she realized how strong their current eye contact was. She took in the sight of his handsome face and the way his eyes sparkled with desire. Her mouth became moist, and before she knew it, he leaned down toward her.

He pressed a gentle kiss to her forehead which instantly warmed her heart. Bakari didn't know exactly what evoked him to kiss her, but he had a sudden impulse and acted on it without even thinking twice about it. Seeing as she didn't protest and only shut her eyes made Bakari plant another peck on her soft skin. Indira couldn't help but smile to herself when his lips landed on her skin again. Then a third peck came on her forehead followed by a kiss on top of her brow.

Indira's eyes fluttered back open, and she realized two things. Firstly, how his lips were moving down her face, and secondly, how close he was. Better yet, how close his lips were. His dilated eyes were locked on her, and his hands were still stroking her lower back. Bakari gently leaned in his lips to hers and kissed her top lip then slowly pulled back.

When her dilated eyes only stayed sealed on his, Bakari kissed her top lip again, and instead of pulling back this time, he captured her lips in a sensual way.

Their mouths began to hungrily embrace one another. Indira eagerly kissed him back, loving the contact of their lips moving in perfect sync and harmony. It was an unexpected moment, but a moment that she didn't protest against. She took his kisses and gave him back the same momentum that he had given her.

As soon as her lips had parted for him, Bakari saw this as his golden opportunity. What had started off as a gentle and intimate kiss was now rapidly turning into a wet, erotic tongue dance. His tongue was possessive, which Indira undeniably enjoyed. The center of her thighs were burning up, and she felt Bakari slowly push her back into the room, kicking the door closed behind him.

Indira couldn't recall the last time she had been kissed this good. Kissing Javon was okay, but absolutely nothing like this. Javon never had her wanting to climax from a kiss of his lips; he never had her mind spinning with ecstasy from his tongue game. And he definitely couldn't dominate her mouth this well.

Getting a taste of Indira Porter was something that Bakari had believed was a fantasy. A silly, little dream that would never ever happen. Ever. However, this right here was no dream. He was really making out with her at this very moment in time. Their tongue thrusting kiss was only getting more heated by the second and making him rock hard in his pants.

Once Indira felt her legs hit the recliner, she pressed a hand to his hard chest which made him end their sinful kiss. The breath that he had managed to take away filled her lungs. She let it out as she opened her eyes to observe him. The lust in his eyes was unmissable.

Neither one of them said a word. They just watched each other, feeling a ray of emotions by what had just gone down. Bakari slowly looked down at his chest that her left hand was on before looking back up at her. The silence between them was still loud, but it didn't ease down the tension that had grown between them.

Just staring into her eyes and seeing the desire cradled within them, the desire she had for him only, made him want her even more. Her desire made him develop the strong urge to continue to tongue her down, lay her down on that recliner, find something to tie her hands with, and fuck her until the sun came up. Fuck her until the only word she could dare to speak was his name. Fuck her until she came all over his manhood. Fuck her until he came and pulled out from her, only to nut all over her breasts and face. Fuck her until he turned her into his nasty, little bitch.

"Bakari... I..."

Indira didn't even know what to say. What she was doing with this man right now, was wrong. It was wrong, but it felt so good, and she didn't want to stop. She didn't want to stop getting a taste of him. She didn't want to stop being with him in this very moment. But the next few words she uttered out of her mouth made it seem like she no longer wanted this.

"...We should stop."

"Is that what you want?"

Indira's cheeks grew hot as she watched him, and she responded with, "S-Sorry."

She knew he could see right through her words. Stopping was the last thing that she wanted. Anything but stopping their moment would suffice.

"Is that what you want?" he repeated confidently. "For us to stop?"

Indira slowly shook her head no, unknowingly beginning to bite her lips at him.

"What do you want, Indira?" he queried as he moved closer to her so that the small gap between them was now non-existent. Then he bent his head low and positioned his lips right by her ear, inhaling her sweet fragrance. "Tell me what you want."

Indira's heart was racing, and her palms were now sweaty. His whisper had hit a special spot in her body. A special, intimate spot that was now gushing like a water tap.

"'Cause I can tell you what I want," he continued. "Better yet, I can show you exactly what I want."

Indira only felt her panties getting wetter at his seductive words.

"W-What do you want?" Indira nervously asked.

"To get a taste of those lips," he voiced as he moved back so he could look at her again.

"You want to kiss me again?"

He suddenly smirked at her before replying, "Undeniably. But those ain't the lips I'm talkin' 'bout." He placed his hands on her waist before sliding his hand across her back and palming her ass before he landed on the back of her pussy through her jeans. "These lips right here."

Shit.

There wasn't a single ounce of doubt in Indira's mind as her body heated up with his touch. This man had her captivated from his first glance and the first touch of his lips on hers. And it was evident to her from the way her body was reacting that she wanted this man. Every last part of him.

"You gon' let me get a taste, Indira?" he queried with a smile in his eyes as he leaned up away from her ears.

With each passing second, Indira's heart only beat faster, and her panties, by now, were soaked. There was only one answer to Bakari's question, and she knew it too.

"Answer me, Indira."

"Yes," she whispered, feeling her nerves reach overload as he stared her down. "You can taste it."

"Taste what?"

Damn, is he really about to make me say it? Indira shyly kept her eyes glued on his.

"Taste... my pussy," she whispered.

"See, that's the thing, Indira," he began seriously. "I'm not planning to just taste it." Her eyes widened with interest at his words. "I'm devouring every last bit of it. I'm sticking this tongue in you, and I want you to ride it. Ride it 'til you can't fuckin' think straight. Ride it 'til the only thing you moan tonight is my name. Ride it 'til your juices are drowning my mouth. Ride my face like you own that shit. Every last part of it."

Indira let out the breath that she had been holding while hearing him talk. Talking such nasty yet alluring words. Words that only made her more intrigued about him. She gently nodded at him, knowing exactly what they were about to do. At this point, it wasn't something she wanted; it was what she needed.

She continued to look up at him with awe, feeling like she was back in high school. Crushing on her friend's older brother and secretly wishing that he could be hers. But in her mind, back then, she thought that he saw her as nothing but a young girl who was close with his sister. Nothing more, and nothing less. Now her secret fantasy had come true indeed. Bakari Marshall wanted her undoubtedly.

She stepped up so that she was on her tiptoes, allowing herself to reach up and peck his lips. When her lips momentarily landed on his again but then broke away, Bakari leaned down and branded their lips together into a longer, passionate kiss. While their lips stayed joined in perfect harmony, Indira felt Bakari gently grab her waist once again and pull her down to the recliner.

Indira quietly moaned when Bakari's thick lips pulled away from her to land on her neck. They began to work their magic, peppering sweet kisses on her skin and sending shockwaves down Indira's spine.

While he seduced her with his lips, his large hands that had been holding her waist were now slowly moving up her t-shirt until they reached her upper back.

By now, Indira had her eyes shut as she enjoyed Bakari's neck kisses and his touch on her body. He was even beginning to bite on her and lick sexily on her skin. She was on a high that only seemed to be getting stronger. A high she never wanted to come down from.

His palms that were on her upper back, slid up her spine until they reached the back of her neck. Indira was filled with bewilderment as his hands traveled higher up her neck until they were on the back of her head, under her hair. Then she felt one of his hands leave her, and her hair tie was quickly tugged off her ponytail.

Indira's eyes popped open when she felt her ponytail fall, and her hair cascaded around her. Bakari's lips left her flesh, and he looked down at her with a tense, sexual gaze. Instead of speaking up, he reached for both her arms, placing them behind her and holding them close together. Indira's head tilted back when her arms were forced to her back.

"Bakari, what are yo..." Her words trailed off when she felt him place her hair tie over her hands and on her wrists.

"Just relax," he gently coached.

Indira continued to gaze into his mesmerizing, brown eyes, her heart racing with anticipation for his next move.

Bakari's eyes drifted down to her jeans, and before she knew it, he was unbuttoning them and pulling down her front zip. Seeing as her hands were currently tied together, she had no balance to lift herself up, so he gently picked her up. Then he slid her jeans over her thighs until they reached her ankles. Indira lifted each foot, allowing him to pull her jeans completely off her body. Once off, she took her seat again. She stayed watching him closely as he stayed crouched down by her legs. Butterflies fluttered feverishly in her stomach as their eyes remained locked on each other. She felt his hands touch on her thighs, stroking upwards until he reached the center, allowing him to begin to pull down on her black lace panties.

"Bakari..."

Her nerves had reached overload at this point. How was she

allowing a complete stranger to have intimate access to her? A complete, sexy stranger.

Bakari had heard her call out to him, but that hadn't stopped him from carrying on his mission. Indira looked down to see that her panties had passed her thighs and were now heading to her ankles. She had allowed him to get this far, and the enticing look in his eyes only told her that there was no going back.

"What did you say to me?" he asked as he pulled her panties over her ankles until they dropped to the floor.

"Huh?"

"Don't act all shy now," he said as he looked back at her. "What did you say you gon' let me taste, Indira?"

"...Taste my pussy."

"Exactly," he confirmed. "You going back on your words?"

"N-No, bu—"

"But nothing," he affirmed. "You're riding my face, Indira. No running, and no trying to push me away. That's why I've tied your hands back. Now you could easily remove that hair tie, but we both know that's what you're not going to do unless you tryna get punished."

Indira's center only fired up at his words. *Get punished?* She lowkey wanted to find out the meaning behind his words.

Bakari gave her one last glance before focusing back down between her thighs and getting on his knees completely instead of just crouching. He couldn't see her pussy properly yet, because she had her thighs pressed up against each other. But when he reached on her calves, she slowly pulled them open for him, allowing him to have the perfect view of her pussy.

God... it's fuckin' beautiful.

And to him it truly was. It was freshly waxed, leaving it completely bald, and seeing the wetness running out her folds confirmed to him that she wanted this just as bad as he wanted it.

Bakari slipped his hand between her thighs, pressing his fingers between her wet lips.

"Why you so wet?" Bakari looked back up at her while running his thick index and middle finger between her slippery folds, only turning her on further. "Huh? Why you so fuckin' wet, Indira?"

The more his fingers began to work her core, the more Indira's libido heightened. He had barely started, but already he had her under his powerful spell.

"Answer me," he demanded, rubbing his fingers faster over her folds before dipping both fingers into her.

"Because... because of you, uhh," she gently moaned.

Unbeknownst to Indira, those three little words were the three words that managed to unleash the beast within Bakari Marshall.

Indira watched with surprise as Bakari lifted both her thighs to his shoulders and thrusted his head deep between her center. The next few moments that quickly followed were an ecstasy like no other.

One thing that Indira hadn't been expecting was this. She had only received head once in this lifetime from Javon. Javon, who confidently told her that he was gonna give her the best head of her life, then ate her like he was trying to suck porridge off a table. After that bad experience, she never bothered to ask him to give her head again. But Bakari, right now, right here, had blown that first bad experience completely away.

His long tongue flicked quickly against her clit, and Indira stared down at him curiously thinking that this was about to be a repeat of her first bad experience, until his wet flesh suddenly thrusted into her tightness. In and out, he maneuvered her opening, providing her with an instant pleasure. The faster he went, the better it felt, and it made Indira finally realize his words from before. Riding his tongue was exactly what he had intended for her to do.

"Oh my... shit!"

Indira's breathing quickened with each push of his tongue. To know that he was really fucking her with his tongue truly blew her mind right now. She had the sudden urge to grab the back of his head, but then she remembered where her hands were and who had put them there.

Bakari groaned into her, releasing his tongue out of her only to roll her juices that lingered in his mouth on her soaked folds.

"You taste... so mothafuckin' good," he complimented her in

between his groans, keeping a firm grasp on her thighs that were locked beside his head.

He licked, sucked, and lapped on her pussy, loving the love faces she was making for him right now. She was also fighting a losing battle with herself right now because from the way her arms were fidgeting behind her, he knew she wanted to release herself.

"Don't you dare," he warned her lightly. "Don't get fucked up, Indira." Then he dipped his tongue back inside her and kept fucking her with his tongue again.

Indira only whimpered louder, feeling the pressure within her grow stronger. She truly couldn't believe it. A man that she didn't even really know was soon going to make her climax from his tongue alone.

"Bakari, please... ahhhh!"

Bakari's entire mouth latched onto her pussy, and his tongue showed no attempts at slowing down. Not bold enough to move her hands, Indira settled on trying to shift her body back so she could somehow escape away from his merciless tongue. But Bakari caught onto her from the second she tried it. He lifted his mouth off her, only to ease two fingers into her slit.

"Oh, so you tryna run, huh?"

"Bak... Bakari..." Trying to speak back to him was a pointless task because she couldn't formulate actual sentences. All she found herself doing was moaning his name louder.

"You tryna fuckin' run, Indira?"

"Bakari... shit, please."

"Please, what?" he asked, a smirk forming on his lips as he observed her creaming all over his fingers with each push inside her.

"Slow... slow... er, ughh!"

"You know better than to ask me that shit, Indira," he said with a light chuckle. "I'm not fuckin' slowing down 'til you cum in my mouth, and even then, I'm still not slowing down. So shut the fuck up and ride my face."

And after saying his last words, Bakari's tongue dove back into her, filling her mind with pure euphoria. She had only gotten high off weed one time, and she knew that this moment right now mimicked that high. Tears started to fill her eyes, and her thighs began to tremble uncontrollably. This man right here had reached a part of her soul that not even her fiancé could.

My fiancé? I'm eng... shit.

And that's when Indira had remembered her situation. Her *big* situation that had completely slipped her mind. She was engaged and getting married in four days. But here she was, letting another man devour her like he was the one that had the right to. Like he was the one allowed to make love to her pussy.

Chapter Five

"T, I know this is hard to s—"

"Hard!" Tokyo yelled as she paced up and down the middle of her salon. "My salon is in ruins!" She let out a crazy laugh as she glanced at a smashed mirror. "I'm going to jail tonight. I'm going to fuckin' jail!"

"You're not going anywhere," Bakari told her as he watched her closely. Still, she paced back and forth while eyeing her shop with hatred and disgust. Hatred and disgust at who had ruined her hard work. "I'm going to handle it."

"Handle it by delivering that nigga's head to me on a silver platter," Tokyo fumed.

"Done."

His response made her stop pacing and turn to look at him with a surprised look. Why she was surprised, she didn't even know. She knew her brother very well and what he was capable of doing. Bakari was a straightforward man, and if he said he was getting something done, then it would done.

"T, next time you decide to have the random urge to spray paint a nigga's car, you let me know. Creating new enemies isn't smart, T, not at all," he warned her lightly. "Lè ou konnen ke niggas pral fè mal ou jwenn nan m '(*When you know that niggas will hurt you to get at me*)."

Tokyo lightly sighed as she listened to his words. As right as he was, Tokyo couldn't help how she felt. She couldn't stop her crazy.

Waking up this morning for work and receiving an urgent text message from Bakari to call her had her worried. She was scared that something had happened to their parents or Arjana. But no. Something worse had happened. Her salon had been vandalized while Indira was locked in her work room.

When Bakari went on to explain further how the intruders had tried to break into Indira's work room, Tokyo was only infuriated further by Carl's crimes. Death seemed like too much of a forgiving punishment, and she felt he deserved much worse. Especially because he had tried to burn down her shop. If it hadn't been for Bakari coming down to check on the salon like he usually did, The Slay Spot would be no more, and Indira? Only God knows what could have happened to her.

Tokyo made sure to call Indira and find out if she was alright before briefly explaining that someone who she used to mess around with had decided to mess around with her place of business. Nonetheless, Tokyo would ensure that they would pay. Then once their call was over, she raced over to the salon where Bakari was already situated. He had made a few calls and gotten a team assembled who would be coming in the next hour to repair Tokyo's salon completely. One thing he wasn't about to have was Tokyo's spot in ruins for more than twenty-four hours. He had given the team a deadline, and he wanted the task of making the salon look good as new completely promptly.

The next thing that Tokyo needed to do was call her workers and let them know that the salon would be closed for the rest of the week. As much as she didn't want to tell them what had gone down, she knew that lying wasn't smart. News in Atlanta spread like a wildfire, so it was only best she came clean and told them that the salon had been vandalized.

"I'll let you know next time I'm on one of my crazy agendas," Tokyo promised simply. "Thank you for being there for me, Kari."

"It's nothing," he said with a neutral look. "That's what I'm here for."

"And thank you for coming to Indi's rescue," she commented,

remembering about her friend. "What she would have done without you... I don't even want to think about what could have happened instead."

Bakari eyed her carefully as his thoughts drifted to Indira. He hadn't been able to stop thinking about her all night. After the moment they had shared? Bakari knew that he wasn't going to ever get her out of his head.

To know that he had gotten a taste of her, had her moaning his name and riding his face, brought him a happiness like no other. Sleeping had been difficult because trying to sleep with a hard on was impossible. And to only wake up even harder than when he had fell asleep was even more challenging.

Last night had been a wonderful night; Bakari couldn't deny it. An unexpected night, but a wonderful night nonetheless. A night that he wouldn't mind experiencing more times. However, with the way Indira had rushed out of the salon once he had made her climax a couple times, with a look of guilt and embarrassment, had Bakari thinking that there was something up with her.

Maybe she's involved with someone? He had a hunch that she was in a relationship, but he didn't bother to ask her because, quite frankly, he didn't care. Temptation filled him a little when talking to Tokyo about her, but it quickly faded. If he didn't know about it already, then clearly that nigga wasn't important.

Thoughts of Indira consumed his mind completely, and he wasn't able to shake her off, not that he wanted to anyway. Indira Porter was in the exact same boat as him because trying to forget about the man that had ate her like a pink Starburst last night was not possible.

He was the only man on her mind as she fell asleep beside Javon last night. Waking up this morning and thinking that she would be able to turn around to see Bakari's handsome face was a thought that had her ashamed. The ring that she had been trying to find before the intruders came into Tokyo's Slay Spot had been found, only making her feel guiltier about her acts with Bakari last night.

You're getting married in three days, but here you are thinking about another man? Pull yourself together, Indira.

It was worse enough that she had kissed him. But for her to let him give her head? In her mind, she had cheated. It may not have been actual sexual intercourse, but kissing another man that wasn't Javon so passionately like that? Allowing him to feast between her legs? That was unacceptable. A small part of herself wanted to take the whole night back, but with how enjoyable it all was, she knew that she didn't want to take it back. She lowkey wanted to experience it again.

"Babe, I need to go run a few errands," Javon's voice sounded, making Indira turn in bed to look at the doorway where he stood fully dressed and ready to go. "Can I use your Uber account to get around?"

"Sure," she quietly said before shutting her eyes and allowing thoughts of Bakari to fill her mind again.

"A'ight, cool. I'll see you later."

Even looking Javon in the eyes this morning was something that she struggled to do. The guilt inside of her wasn't disappearing, and it seemed that the more she looked at Javon, the more she wished it was Bakari. She had never had thoughts like this before. Ever. Not a single man had been able to make her want him as bad as Bakari now had.

Yes, back in her high school days, she could happily admit that she had a little crush on him. But who didn't? Bakari Marshall was the epitome of fine. If a girl didn't have a little interest in him, then something was considered wrong with her. However, when high school was over and she met Javon, Bakari became a distant memory. A distant memory that she chose to forget all about until she got back in contact with Tokyo Marshall and started working for her.

Seeing him once managed to evoke those high school feelings again. But Indira convinced herself that they were nothing and suppressed them well. The only thing she was unable to stop was the flutter in her heart and butterflies in her stomach when she saw him. Now they had crossed a boundary that wasn't supposed to be crossed, and those high school feelings were no longer trying to be hidden. They wanted to be set free whether Indira liked it or not.

How could I let that happen?

She hadn't even told Javon what had happened last night in the salon with the intruders. A part of her didn't want him to fuss about it since it was over, but another part of her didn't want to bring up the fact that Bakari had saved her. She knew her man well, and if he knew that *the* Bakari Marshall had saved his woman, his ego would be shattered.

I just need to forget about him for good. He's not Javon... But honestly, I think I need to tell Javon the truth about what we did... But if I come clean, that could be the end of us. Okay, but you've dealt with his infidelities in the past before, Indira. Can't he just deal with this one-time mistake?

It was true. Javon had slipped up a couple times in their relationship. A couple times had been an exact two times. The first time was with this girl that Indira had caught him sexting at the start of them moving in together in their current home. The second time was at a night out with his boys. Javon had claimed that he had gotten too drunk and accidentally let a stripper "suck his dick for five minutes." Indira was obviously smarter than that and knew there was more to the story. And that was because the stripper ended up being one of her clients and told her the entire story. Javon had been the one feeling all up on her and offered to pay for her services for the entire night, which she happily accepted because, after all, money was money to her. He wasn't drunk either and completely sober.

However, Javon pleaded and won back Indira's affection over the course of four months. He even cried to her, promising to never do anything with another woman but her. So Indira forgave him and let him move back in with her.

He had slipped up twice and she had only slipped up once. So surely, he had to forgive her. Indira wanted to come clean about this situation because she wasn't sure she could take this down the aisle or to the grave. She wasn't one to keep secrets away from Javon, and with how much their relationship had improved over the last year, he never kept secrets from her.

Should I tell hi...

H.E.R.'s voice suddenly filled the room, interrupting her thoughts.

> *But I don't wanna give up*
> *Baby, I just want you to get up*
> *Lately I've been a little fed up*
> *Wish you would just focu—*

"Hi, Mom," Indira said simply as she picked up her phone on the second ring.

"Indira," her mother greeted her nonchalantly. "I need a favor... I'm going out tonight and I need you to babysi—"

"Babysit Noah," Indira cut her off.

"Yeah. Can you?"

Indira's relationship with her mother was somewhat... complicated. It didn't help that her mother had her when she was only sixteen. Her late brother, Kieran, had come into the world when Indira turned four. So not only was Siobhan an inadequate mother, she preferred living the same exact lifestyle that had gotten her pregnant: being a party girl.

Now at the age of forty, Siobhan Porter was still very much a party girl. Age wasn't nothing but a number in her eyes, and it wasn't about to stop her from living her best life until the day she departed from this earth.

Her looks helped her very much because, despite her age, Siobhan didn't look a day past twenty-six. So she used that to her advantage when prancing around town, hitting up all the hottest clubs and bars with her friends. Hitting up all the hottest clubs and bars with her friends frequently left her broke and crying on Indira's doorstep, begging for her help. Because that was her mother, Indira wasn't about to abandon her. When she first lost her apartment over two years ago, Indira let her move in with her temporarily until she got back on her feet. Once finding a new rich baller to finance her, Siobhan bounced and didn't speak to her daughter for six months, only to return back on her doorstep with a baby bump.

"Sure," Indira replied, more than happy to babysit her brother tonight. "What time?"

"I'll be dropping him off in an hour."

Indira's face scrunched up with confusion as she pulled her phone down to her eye level to look at her clock which said 3:40 p.m.

"Mom, it's not even 6 p.m. yet. Why ar—"

"I've got shit to do, and I need to get ready! Just be ready to take him in an hour."

And after saying that, Siobhan ended the call without even letting Indira get another word in.

Noah may have been her half-brother, but she loved him with all her heart. He was only three years old, and finding out that her mother was pregnant by some random man wasn't a big shock to Indira. As much as her mother liked partying, she loved men even more. Rich men to be exact. If your pockets were stacked and you could spoil her rotten, Siobhan would give you a first-class VIP access into sliding between her thighs. Her mother was a lot, but over the course of her life, Indira had learned to deal with it.

Indira was pissed that her mother had ambushed her like this, knowing that she wouldn't say no. But she was also glad to have her brother's company, because he would be a good distraction.

An hour later, Indira's doorbell rang, and she went to open it, only to have Noah thrusted into her arms and her mother rushing away.

"Bye, baby. Don't give your sister too much trouble!" Siobhan yelled before opening up the car door of a Bentley and getting in.

Indira watched as the car sped off down the street before turning to look into the innocent brown eyes of her brother.

"I guess it's just you and I, little man," Indira announced lovingly as she pecked his cheek. "You hungry?"

Noah quickly nodded and rested his forehead against his sister's chest as she led them into her home.

One of the reasons why Indira was so accepting toward her half-brother, despite not knowing who his father was, was because having a brother again, after losing her first one, greatly warmed her heart. She loved Kieran greatly and always wanted to look out for him. Unfortunately, the car crash that had taken his life had been unexpected, and Indira was unable to protect her brother because he was now dead. When Noah came into the world, she made it her priority to ensure that she looked out for him no matter what. So even though her mother took advantage of Indira's soft spot for Noah, Indira didn't mind too much. Noah was family, and that was all that mattered to her.

Indira and Noah spent the rest of the day eating, playing, and watching animated children movies that Noah loved. While watching movies, Indira's thoughts drifted back to Bakari until she reminded herself of her wedding in three days.

I honestly think you need to call the wedding off... or postpone this for a later date. You can't get married when you have thoughts of wanting another man, Indira. What sense does that make? ... I love Javon, but... I don't know. I just need to talk to him about this whole wedding.

Indira looked at the clock to see that it was 9 p.m. It was getting late, and Javon hadn't returned home yet. He hadn't even called or texted her to let her know where he was. But what she did notice was how her email was blowing up with receipts from Uber. Receipts that added up to 150 dollars. As the hours continued to pass and it got to midnight, Indira only filled with more rage about Javon not being home yet. She tried to call him, but his phone went straight to voicemail, worrying her further.

Where the hell is he?

After putting Noah to sleep, Indira started going through her contacts, trying to find the number to Javon's best friend, Malcom. When about to call his line, an incoming call popped up on her screen from an unknown number. Unknown numbers always made her hesitant, and she rarely picked up. But something about this particular unknown caller made her resist the urge to ignore the call.

"Hello?"

"Indi, baby."

Hearing Javon's voice come on the line made her frown.

"Where the hell are you, Javon? I've been calling and texting your phon—"

"My phone died, Indi," he explained in an apologetic tone. "Something's happened."

"What?"

"My father had a stroke," Javon announced gravely. "I've been in the hospital with him all day, Indi... He almost died."

Chapter Six

J avon's father had indeed suffered from a mini stroke. If it hadn't been for Javon getting to his father when he had, then things would have been much worse. Now Indira felt guilty for snapping over the phone at Javon last night. He was going through it, but she had been inconsiderate.

Javon's father was still in the hospital and being watched, but he had a few physical conditions with his balance, weakness, and fatigue. Because of his condition, he wasn't going to be able to attend their wedding, and that more than anything made Javon depressed.

"So I guess what I'm tryna say is," Javon announced with a dulled expression, "I want us to push the wedding back."

Relief suddenly filled into Indira's heart as she stared into Javon's eyes. Relief should have been the last emotion that Indira felt, but she couldn't help it.

"And I know how excited we both are to get married, but I don't want to get married without my dad being present. And because of his stroke, he won't be able to do much by himself, so I really want to move in with him for a while... I just want to make sure that he's well taken care of. I know we're going to lose the money we paid to the courthouse and for the honeymoon, but I can't do this without my dad."

Indira's face instantly softened into an understanding look.

"Pushing back the wedding is fine, love," she agreed. "I know you want your father present, and I want him there too. We can't get married without him, so him getting back in great shape is the main priority."

Javon gave her a large smile and grabbed her hand.

"See, this is why I love you so much. You're so understanding," he concluded before leaning forward toward her and branding their lips together.

So it was settled then. They would be pushing their wedding back for three months, allowing Javon's father to recover fully from his stroke and get back to a good health.

While Javon packed up some of his things that he would need while staying with his father, Indira made a call to her god sister, letting her know that the wedding was being pushed back. Emaza was upset to hear the wedding was being postponed and wished Javon's father a quick recovery. She also decided that instead of flying in tomorrow for the wedding as planned, she would fly in next week in order to spend some quality time with Indira. Indira happily agreed, loving the sound of that. Then it was time for her to let her mother know.

She had already seen Siobhan in the early hours of the morning when she came to collect Noah. Indira rang her, but unfortunately, she didn't pick up the phone, so Indira sent her a text message explaining the situation. Calling Tokyo proved to be the same result, because she didn't pick up. So Indira sent her a text and hoped her response came in soon. Fifteen minutes later, it finally did.

Tokyo: *Awww love, I'm so sorry to hear about your fiance's father. And I'm sorry I missed your call. I was sorting something out. You okay though?*

Indira: *Yeah just fine. I'll be back to start work again.*

Tokyo: *Great! The salon's back open next week.*

Tokyo: *And I've taken extra precautions to ensure that what happened won't happen ever again. I'm really sorry that you were placed in that position.*

Indira: *It's fine, honestly. I'm just glad to be alive... and I'm thankful that Bakari was able to save me.*

Tokyo: *Me too girl!*

Tokyo: *See you next week back at the shop x*

Indira: *Next week indeed! x*

Tokyo: *Hey... since you're not getting married on Friday anymore than means you're free, right?*

Indira: *Yeah I guess. Why, what's up?*

Tokyo: *My sister's boss is reopening up his tattoo spot after getting it renovated. He's throwing a party in the new shop and I figured that since you don't have anything better to do, you could come down?*

Tokyo: *You could even invite Javon.*

Indira: *He's not really much of a party person...*

Tokyo: *What about you?*

Tokyo: *You and I used to turn up back in the day.*

Indira: *We did indeed.*

Tokyo: *And it was fun! So come on Friday, get some liquor in you and enjoy the night with me.*

Indira: *Honestly with this wedding now pushed back and with the days I still have off all I really want to do is sleep.*

Indira: *But thanks so much for the invite, boss lady. I appreciate it a lot.*

Tokyo: *No worries. The offer still stands though.*

Indira took one last glance at Tokyo's text message before locking her phone. Partying wasn't really on her agenda right now. With the wedding pushed back and Javon moving out to live with his father for a while, Indira knew that life was about to get laborious. She was going to need to announce that she was back working at Tokyo's Slay Spot, and once that happened, her inbox would be full with emails. But before she made that announcement, her main focus would be to help Javon pack and make sure that he was okay. Because she knew how worried he was about his father and his health.

"How you feeling, love?" Indira asked Javon as she folded his clothes into a neat pile.

"Worried," Javon mumbled as he sat on the edge of their bed with a sorrowful expression. "I know he's still in the hospital right now, but I really don't want to leave his side."

"I know, babe. I know."

Javon's father would be discharged out of the hospital in three days and be back home where Javon would have moved some of his stuff into in order to look after him.

"He's going to be so happy to have you supporting him twenty-four-seven," Indira said with a loving smile. "He's so lucky to have a son like you, Von."

"Thank you, Indi..." Javon's words trailed off quietly, and when he turned away from her, Indira could automatically sense that something was up. So she stopped folding his t-shirt, sauntered over to him, and took a seat next to him.

"What's wrong?" she innocently asked as she playfully nudged his shoulder.

Javon looked up at her before giving her a weak smile.

"Nothing..." Indira gave him an unconvinced look which managed to make his smile strengthen. "Okay... Well, I'm just pissed that I don't have a whip to get around in. If I had a car, I could easily move my stuff to my father's house without depending on your Uber account... It just sucks, man."

Indira listened carefully to his words, sympathizing with him greatly. But using her Uber account was fine with her as long as he didn't run up the bill again like he had yesterday.

"I'm fi—"

"No, Indira. I don't want you to do that," Javon interrupted her. "It's too much."

"Do what?" She gave him a look of pure confusion, but he chose to overlook it.

"Buy me a car," he said. "I mean, it would be great, and I wouldn't have to depend on your Uber account anymore. But it's too much, baby. You really don't have to."

Buying Javon a car was the last thing on Indira's mind. She was just about to assure him that him using her Uber account to get around was fine.

"Babe, using my Uber account is fine," she explained. "You're going to be with your father all the time anyways, so you'll hardly use my account unless you're coming back home to me."

Javon's softened look quickly began to harden as he looked at her.

"But I'll be going on errands for my dad and most likely take him out of the house. A car would relieve a lot of stress. You know that."

"I just don't see the need for it," she admitted with a light shrug. "It is too much, like you stated, and besides, you won't be going out all the ti—"

"Yes I wi..." Javon silenced himself and decided to ease down his forceful tone. "You know what? Forget it," he concluded before getting up from their bed and walking out the room.

Indira didn't get why he was now in a foul mood. She hadn't been the one to bring up getting him a car in the first place. He had been. And still, she didn't see the need for one. Why would he need a car when he had nowhere to drive to?

Ding!

Indira looked down at the vibrating phone next to her.

+678 831 5459: *I really miss sitting on your face.... I know you have a girl but that ain't st—*

"You going through my phone now?"

Indira hadn't been able to read the rest of the text because Javon, who had come back into their bedroom, snatched his phone off the bed. She stared up at him with a perplexed look.

"I'm sorry."

"You going through my phone now? You don't trust me?"

"Javon, you see me sitting here and know damn well I didn't lay a finger on your phone," she snapped. "But that's not the point. Who's texting you, Javon?"

Javon took a peek at his phone only to unlock his phone and tap on his screen, making Indira fill with rage.

"Nah, don't start deleting shit now!" she yelled at him, watching him stay glued to his phone as he walked away from her. "Who the hell is texting you right now, Javon? So you're fucking chea..." Her words trailed off when Javon sauntered back toward her and thrusted his phone in her face.

His screen read:

+678 831 5459: *I really miss sitting on your face... I know you have a girl but that ain't stop you the last time.*

Javon: *Who the fuck is this?*

+678 831 5459: *Omari?*

Javon: *Who the fuck is that?*

+678 831 5459: *OMG! Wrong number. So sorry!*

A wave of guilt filled Indira as she examined his bright screen. Here she was again, thinking only about herself. Her eyes darted back up to his chestnut irises only to see the knowing look in his eyes. However, instead of snapping on her like she had snapped on him, he decided to place his phone away and take a seat back next to her. Then he wrapped his arms around her, placing her close and stroking her.

"I'm sorry," Indira apologized, tears filling her eyes.

"It's okay, love. I get it. I've messed up in the past, so I know seeing that would trigger you. I'm the sorry one."

"No, no," Indira disagreed, pulling herself out of his arms so she could look at him. "I'm sorry. I'm so sorry."

Javon looked at her with surprise, completely baffled at why she was apologizing so much. She had only lashed out at him because of what she had seen on his phone. But deep down, Indira knew why she was apologizing to him. Because of what she had done to him. Cheating on him with...

"I'll buy you the car," Indira announced enthusiastically.

"What? Bae, no, you don't have t—"

"I want to," she voiced seriously. "I want to."

He grinned at her before pecking her lips. "I..." Another peck followed. "Love..." And another one. "You."

A small smile graced her lips before she asked, "What car do you want?"

"Anything really... something simple. I don't really mind. I know whatever you choose for me will be amazing."

- Two Days Later -

Staring up at her white ceiling was calming indeed for Indira. It felt relaxing to not have to apply any eyelashes on clients for the past two days. All she had been doing was sleeping, eating, and of course, she had bought Javon a brand-new ride.

A 2018 Audi A5 Coupe to be exact. It had been the car that he had been admiring greatly, constantly talking about, and walking past. It had cost her just under $60,000, and seeing that she could afford to buy the car without putting a down payment, she bought it in full. It took a huge chunk of out her savings, but it was nothing she couldn't earn back. Her man now had a car and was happy. That was all that mattered.

With Javon now not around, she had plenty of personal time, and with that came constant thoughts of Bakari Marshall. She didn't like that he was still on her mind 24/7. Her belief had been that after buying Javon the car, her conscience would be clear, and all thoughts of Bakari would be out of the window. However, things had only gotten worse. That night they shared was like a constant replay in her mind, and as much as she attempted to block it out, she just could not.

Was it wrong that she wanted to experience the feel of his lips again?

Of course it's wrong, Indira! You may not be getting married today, but you're still engaged. Engaged she still was. Javon pushing the wedding back didn't mean that they weren't going to tie the knot. It only meant that it wouldn't be happening right now.

She was actually surprised at how laid back and understanding she had been about Javon postponing the wedding. It wasn't something that she actually saw as a big deal because they still planned to get married. Just not now. What was the point of putting up a fight over a situation that she understood completely? Javon's father was his world, and without him present, there would be no wedding. She got that wholeheartedly. However, a deeper part of Indira knew exactly why she hadn't put up a fight about the wedding. She just chose not to address it.

Javon would spend Monday to Fridays with his father while his brother who worked full time took over from him Saturday to Sunday. That meant that Javon would only sleep in their apartment on Saturday nights and leave Sunday night to tend back to his father.

The one thing that bothered Indira was the fact that Javon still didn't have a job. He would be looking after his father for the entire week, so how would he able to work?

Indira knew she was going to have to bring it up, but for now, she would leave it be. Javon needed to stay focused on his father, and that was that. She was already paying the entire rent, so it was just something she was going to have to keep dealing with for the time being.

Ding!

Indira turned her head to the side to lay eyes on her phone that was now lit up as it sat on her lamp stand. She reached over to pick it up and spotted Tokyo's name on her screen.

Tokyo: *Still not in a partying mood?*

Indira quickly unlocked her phone and typed back: *No, but I have a feeling you're about to make me get into one.*

Tokyo's response was swift: *You know it!*

Tokyo: *Come on! It'll be fun.*

Tokyo: *I'll come pick you up at 9:30? The grand opening's at 7:45 and then the party starts at 8.*

Indira: *So why aren't you going earlier?*

Tokyo: *Where's the fun in that? Bad bitches show up late and make a real entrance.*

Indira sent her a few laughing emojis.

Tokyo: *So it that a yes?*

Indira sighed softly as she stared at her phone clock. The time was now 4 p.m. which meant she had plenty of time to get ready for the party. She could even throw in another nap if she felt like it. Today was supposed to be the day she got married, but here she was in bed like a loner.

Indira: *Yes.*

Tokyo: *Yaaaaaaaaay!*

Tokyo: *Wear some real sexy shit tonight girl. I know you're taken and all that but ain't nothing wrong with showing niggas what they can't have.*

Indira: *What kind of sexy shit?*

Tokyo: *The type of sexy shit that would make me, a girl who only loves dick, want to get a taste of you.*

Indira smirked at her response before texting back: *Got it, boss lady.*

After sending her last text message, Indira decided to head to her wardrobe and find something to wear.

It took her hours, but she finally settled on something, and when the clock hit 7 p.m., she started to beat her face with makeup and get dressed. Tokyo ended up arriving quite late. What was supposed to be a pick-up time of 9:30 p.m. turned into 10:45 p.m.

"Indira! Girlllllllllll," Tokyo excitedly sang as she watched Indira walk away from her locked front door. "Forget the party. Let's just head back to my place noooow!"

Indira giggled shyly at Tokyo's remark and opened her passenger side door before getting in.

"Thank you, boss lady. You're looking beautiful yourself," Indira complimented her as she eyed her red strapless dress.

Tokyo gave her a sweet smile before stating, "Sorry I took so long. I would blame it on the traffic, but in reality, it's really just me."

Indira cracked an amused grin at Tokyo and watched as she put the car in gear and pulled off from the front of Indira's home.

They arrived at their destination half an hour later, and Tokyo parked her i8 in an available parking spot a short distance away from the tattoo shop. Then they walked together to the shop where they could hear loud music blasting from.

The closer they got to the entrance, Indira could feel an empty feeling in the pit of her stomach, and her breathing quickened. She had the sudden desire to run away, but when Tokyo grabbed her hand and led them past a group of people smoking weed outside the shop, she knew there was no going back. They entered the tattoo shop, and all eyes were immediately on them.

"T!" Tokyo heard her sister before seeing her. She turned to the side only to see Arjana quickly walking toward her with a grin plastered on her face. "Finally, you made it!"

Tokyo laughed awkwardly and let go of Indira's hand to embrace her sister.

"You look great, sis," Arjana complimented her while they embraced before her eyes drifted to Indira. "Who's your pretty friend?"

"Indira, this is my gorgeous sister, Arjana," Tokyo spoke up once their embrace was over. "Arjana, this pretty lady is Indira."

"Ohhhh, so you're the lady hooking up everyone with the bomb ass lashes? It's nice to be able to put a face to a name."

Indira gave her a friendly smile before replying, "It's nice to finally meet you too."

"Let's get you two a drink ASAP," Arjana voiced as she began walking deeper into the shop. "Come on."

Tokyo willingly followed her sister, and Indira had no choice but to do the same, avoiding the hard gaze of many eyes she could feel.

From what she could see so far, the tattoo shop looked good. It had a color scheme of dark red, white, and black. Artistic paintings were hung up on its white walls, and dark red furniture graced the store. The shop had two floors, because at the back of it was a staircase leading upstairs. There were also various tattoo booths, and the waiting area which Indira and Tokyo had come in through was packed with guests.

People were either dancing to the upbeat music, drinking away, or having conversations with each other. And the shop seemed to be getting fuller with more people by the second.

"Hey, guys!" Arjana announced once making it to the back of the shop where the drinks were. "Look who finally decided to show up, and she brought a guest."

Indira slowly looked up, only to lock eyes with the one man she wasn't expecting to see right now. He had a drink to his lips, but upon laying eyes on her, he lifted it off his mouth and placed all his attention on her.

Fuck, she looks gorgeous.

Indira was wearing a black dress and black heels to match. But this dress right here was not just any simple old black dress. It was a tight-fitting dress that hugged her body perfectly. It had a deep plunge neck-line which gave a perfect view of her cleavage sitting upright and pretty. It was as if the dress had been crafted just for her with only her shape in mind. Her hair was up in a ponytail away from her face, making her gorgeous features stand out more. The more Bakari stared at her, the more he wanted to eat her up. Better yet, pull up that dress of hers, open up her thighs, and eat that pu—

"Sorry I'm late, Yasir," Tokyo greeted Yasir in an apologetic tone. "Traffic and all." She stepped closer toward him so that she could embrace him. "The shop looks amazing."

"Thank you, T," he replied as they hugged. "Who's your friend?"

"This is my beautiful friend and employee, Indira Porter." Tokyo introduced Indira, giving her an excited grin. "Indi, this is Yasir, the owner of the tattoo spot and Bakari's good friend."

Yasir was handsome indeed. He was a chocolate man with a low-cut head of waves, full beard, and a thick moustache around his pink, plump lips. Peeking out from under his navy, satin shirt was a flesh full of tattoos. He stood at six feet one and had a muscular physique. Indira stared into his hooded mahogany eyes and beamed at him.

"Nice to meet you. Congratulations on reopening your shop. It looks great."

"Appreciate it, love," Yasir thanked her pleasantly.

At the back of the shop where Arjana had led her sister and Indira, was Bakari, Yasir, and a bunch of Yasir's homies. Bakari was situated in the middle of the men whereas they stood around him. He gave off the vibe of him being the leader, and Indira was turned on completely by that shit. However, to have all these men, including Bakari, staring at her made Indira feel intimidated. She wasn't used to having this many eyes on her, especially male eyes.

Sensing Indira's apprehensive state when she glanced at her, Tokyo decided it was best they grabbed a drink and went somewhere else. Tokyo quickly poured them both a glass of Bacardi rum, orange juice, then pineapple juice, and then led Indira back toward the main area where everyone was.

"Thank you," Indira whispered to her once they were away from the back of the shop.

"No problem, girl. You know I got you," Tokyo promised. "Now drink up, and get ready to shake that booty of yours all night."

Indira giggled before doing as Tokyo asked and took a large gulp from her red cup.

Now I like dollars, I like diamonds
I like stunting, I like shining
I like million-dollar deals
Where's my pen? Bitch, I'm signin'

As soon as the song changed to Cardi B's "I Like It", all the ladies in the shop started going crazy and formed a huddle in the center of the dancefloor. Tokyo grabbed Indira and led her to the huddle so they could turn up together. All the girls happily rapped along to the song and danced away together.

By now, Bakari had heard the loud noise of rapping coming from the main area, and that made him walk back into the main room only to marvel at the sight of Indira enjoying herself. She was dancing away without a single worry in the world, and to see her looking so damn attractive while she did it turned him on in the worst way. He stayed watching her for a few more minutes, noticing her catch a quick glance at him before quickly looking away from him. It only made him smirk to himself before deciding to go off somewhere and chill by himself. One thing Bakari hated was parties, but to show his support to Yasir, he decided to come out tonight.

"Babe, I'm gonna pee real quick," Tokyo stated thirty minutes later after the girls were becoming tired of constantly dancing.

"Girl, me too," Indira voiced.

"Alrightie, let's go then."

Tokyo grabbed Indira's hand and led the way to the restrooms upstairs on the second floor. They entered the fragrant smelling room, and each took an empty cubicle. What was an empty restroom started filling up a few seconds later when Indira heard female voices.

"Girl, did you see her?"

"Of course I did." The second female laughed. "Almost every guy in here is lusting over her dumb ass."

Indira's eyes perked up as their conversation continued.

"Girl, aren't you fucking her man?"

"I sure am. Every single night I can," the second female confirmed. "Girl, he even made me act a fool while texting him the other day. I texted him talking about I miss sitting on your face, hit me up. But I texted at a wrong time because he texted back, pretending not to know me, and he's coached me on situations like this. If he texts me back 'Who the fuck is this?' then I gotta play dumb and act like I don't know his ass."

"For real? Damn, that's some real smart, sneaky shit."

"I know right," the second female replied happily. "I just can't wait for him to leave her ass for good and just be with me. He knows who the right woman is, and it's clearly me."

"I'm sure soon enough he'll come to his senses."

"And I'll happily steer him into the right direction," the second female explained. "You know how good I am at persuasion."

"Oh yeah, I know. You and that weapon between your thighs... making niggas of Atlanta go crazy."

"You know it, girl!" She laughed, and the first female laughed alongside her.

Tokyo had peed already and washed her hands. She simply ignored the females gossiping about one of them sleeping with someone's man and wondered why Indira was taking so long. "Indira! You done in there?"

The two females' hysterical laughter continued and echoed out of the room as they left the restroom.

Without a doubt in her mind, Indira knew exactly who those two girls were talking about. The female's story matched perfectly to the story that Indira had in her head. The story of how someone had texted Javon's phone and he had texted back 'Who the fuck is this?' only for her to act dumb like she had texted the wrong number. Indira didn't care about what anyone had to say. Javon had been cheating on her this whole time.

Tears slowly flowed out of Indira's eyes as she began to realize how much of a fool she was. A big fool for falling for Javon's lies. *That conniving, little bast—*

Knock! Knock!

"Indira, you okay in there?"

"...Yeah, I'm okay," she lied, taking a deep breath. "I'm okay... Can you just give me a minute?"

"Sure thing. I'll be right here if you ne—"

Two bad bitches and we kissin' in the Wraith
Kissin'-kissin' in the Wraith, kiss-kissin' in the Wraith

"Ooo, I need to quickly take this call," Tokyo reluctantly announced. "Sorry, hun. I'll be a few minutes."

"No worries, boss lady."

"I'll meet you back downstairs?"

"Sounds like a plan," Indira responded before Tokyo answered her call and rushed out the restroom.

Indira pulled some toilet tissue and began to carefully dab her tears away. She had spent so much time beating her face, and ruining it would only make her more depressed. She couldn't believe it though. Javon was really out here embarrassing her. Embarrassing her with a random Atlanta chick. Javon had been playing her this entire time while he had put a ring on her finger. They were supposed to get married today! Today, she would have been his wife.

Indira looked down at her ring and slowly slid it off her finger. *I'm going to kill him. That's the only solution.* Indira didn't see any other option. He had to die for his betrayal. It didn't matter about what she had done with Bakari when clearly Javon had never stopped cheating.

Indira took a deep breath, coaching herself to calm down and placing her ring into her purse. As mad as she was, this wasn't the place or time. Tonight, she just needed to relax and let her hair down. However, deep down she knew that the night was over. She was no longer in the mood and ready to go. She finally flushed the toilet and made her way out of the cubicle to wash her hands at the sink before heading to the dryer. Once her hands were dry, Indira gave herself one last look in the mirror, making sure she still looked decent. Her tears hadn't altered her makeup, and for that, she was glad.

Even though she had agreed to meet Tokyo back downstairs, she honestly wanted to leave. Knowing that Javon's side piece was at this party, knowing exactly who she was and watching her every move, truly infuriated her. *I'm gonna wait for Tokyo to finish her call and tell her I'm going. I can't stay here anymore,* she mused as she left the restroom. The second floor of the shop was very similar to the first. Like downstairs, the second floor housed more tattoo booths and had a long corridor that led to a fire escape door.

I could use some fresh air in fact, Indira mused to herself as she walked across the corridor to the door. She gently pushed it open, only to fill with elation at the cool breeze that hit her body. Then her elation grew when she realized what this fire escape led to a rooftop that over-looked the breathtaking view of the city.

She stepped forward to get closer to the balcony only to fully examine the area, and that's when she laid eyes on... *him*.

Oh sweet Jesus.

Her heart pounded rapidly as his back faced her, but when he slowly turned around to lay eyes on her, her heart skipped a beat. She had definitely wondered where he had disappeared off to while following Tokyo to the restroom. Originally, she assumed he had gone home, but now she was seeing him again, proving her wrong.

Tonight, he had opted for a beige short sleeved t-shirt and denim Armani jeans with fresh white air force 1's on his feet. A thin gold chain hung around his neck, gold studs locked in each ear, and on his wrist was a matching gold Audemar. A look that would have appeared simplistic on any other guy, but on him, it looked divine. When he lifted his blunt to his lips and inhaled it, Indira watched him with a bated breath, and when he let out the smoke, she breathed out too.

"You can't say hi now?" he asked with a curious look gracing his handsome face before he took one last hit of his weed and chucked it over the balcony.

"Hi," she shyly greeted him, remaining frozen in her stance.

Not feeling the distance between them at all, Bakari took bold strides toward her until he was able to tower over her. As he walked to her, Indira took him in and all his glory. Seeing the way his eyes refused to leave hers as he came toward her, made butterflies fly feverously within her stomach. When he was in front of her, Indira moved out the way for him to pass, but instead of moving past her, he stayed towering over her. She felt like she was floating as they continued to stare each other down, and eventually, Bakari spoke up to kill their silence.

"You couldn't say hi to a nigga before?" he asked her with a curious look.

"...I was nervous when I walked into that area," she admitted shyly. "Besides, your sister was introducing me to Yasir."

"Yeah, but all of that shit ain't got nothing to with why you couldn't say hi to me," Bakari stated boldly.

"My apologies," she quietly responded before breaking eye contact with him to look anywhere but into his cocoa brown irises. Those irises that always knew how to trap her into a powerful, wicked spell. However, the second she tried to look away from him, she felt her chin being pulled back up, and her eyes were back on his.

"You look beautiful tonight."

His compliment made her instantly smile, and his simple touch formed a fire between her thighs.

"Thank you."

"No need to thank me when it's the truth," he explained as he let go of her chin. Indira said nothing in return and just continued to get lost in those eyes of his.

"Enjoy the rest of your night," Bakari concluded, ready to walk past her and completely fight the urge to kiss her like he did last time. Better yet, the urge to get on his knees and taste the sweet nectar between her thighs.

"Bakari..."

Instead of walking past her, he stayed still in his position, intrigued to know what she wanted.

"...What we did... you know... that night..."

"What about it?" he bluntly queried, his eyes piercing into hers.

"... It... It wasn't... suppos—"

"You got a nigga?" he cut her off. "Is that what you tryna tell me?"

She slowly began to nod at him.

"I'm sort of... engaged," she revealed, making his eyes widen slightly.

"Is that right," he commented with lackluster.

"Yeah, we were supposed to get married today, but... the wedding got pushed back."

"I see," Bakari simply responded, wetting his bottom lip as he stared her up and down.

"I just thought I owed it to you to come clean about my situation."

Bakari said nothing, and it made her fill with bewilderment. She expected him to be angry for not revealing that she was someone's wife to be, but he didn't seem to care.

"Doesn't that bother you?"

"Why would it?"

"Because I'm engaged."

"Engaged to a nigga that can't eat your pussy right," he voiced coolly. The word 'pussy' leaving his lips sounded too alluring, and she instantly felt herself get moist down below. "Why would that shit bother me? I should be asking you if you're the one bothered. You're not even wearing your damn ring." Indira immediately turned red with embarrassment at him picking up on that. "He don't even know what to do with all of this." Bakari's eyes darted up and down Indira's body, admiring every last part of it. "All of this sexy ass body of yours..."

Indira felt her breathing catch in her throat when his large palm connected with the back of her dress. Her ass cheeks to be exact. He had given her a light spank and was now rubbing on her butt like he owned it, looking at her hungrily like he owned her.

"Bakari," she lightly whispered his name, feeling her wetness increase. Their eyes stayed sealed on one another, and their tension only grew stronger. "Please..."

"Please, what?" He taunted her as he kept rubbing her butt with both his large palms, and his lips landed on her exposed shoulder, pecking her skin.

"Huh? Please, what?" He pecked along her shoulder until he reached the curve of her neck and was able to seduce her with his lips. The smell of her vanilla scent filled his nostrils, and he felt intoxicated.

"Please don't... don't make me... make me want you again," she whispered with a quiet moan seeping past her lips. The touch of his soft lips on her skin right now was driving her crazy. Completely insane in fact.

"Too bad, Indira. 'Cause that's exactly what I intend to fuckin' do," he boldly snapped before continuing to kiss her skin. "You think I give a fuck about that nigga? That nigga that can't fuck you 'til you can't think straight? That nigga that can't blow your back out properly and get all up in them guts?"

"Bakari, pl—"

"Shut the fuck up, I'm speaking," he ordered as he lightly bit on her flesh, making her whimper. "You never should have let a nigga like me get a taste of you, Indira. 'Cause now that I've had one taste, I don't want to stop tasting you, and quite frankly, I don't intend to stop."

Hearing his words brought her a pleasure like no other, and she was tempted to question him on his desire for her.

"...So you want me?"

"Every last part of you," he confirmed with one last kiss to her neck before leaning up from her neck and looking down at her.

"What if I don't want you?" she challenged him, but instead of answering her, Indira felt his palms move from her butt to slide onto her thighs until his hands disappeared under her dress. They made their way straight to her center and landed on her intimate spot. Indira softly sighed when she felt him rub on her soft middle through her lace panties.

"That's not what she's telling me," Bakari stated with a small smirk as their eyes stayed connected. He pressed into her material only to feel more wetness against his fingers. "That's not what she's telling me at all, Indira."

His fingers started to slowly rub on her soft center, and Indira instinctively shut her eyes, enjoying the pleasure that he brought. Despite the lace material barrier between his fingers and her pussy, he was still making her feel good from his simple yet effective moves. She was only creaming more against her lace as his fingers continued to work their magic, massaging her folds. The more he did it, the more she wanted things to go further between them.

"Let's... Let's go," she said breathlessly, opening her eyes to stare up into his lustful pupils.

"Go where, Indira?"

"Go to wherever you can fuck the shit out of me," she boldly told him. "I want you, Bakari. I want you inside me tonight."

But Bakari couldn't wait. He had to have her now. Without even saying anything, Bakari pulled his hands out from under her black dress before grabbing her hand and pulling her toward the balcony.

"Bakari, what ar... Uh!" Indira gasped loudly when Bakari pushed her against the balcony and pressed his center into her center. Feeling the cold edge of the balcony against her body hadn't bothered her at all. Because what she was more bothered by was how Bakari was pressed up against her, allowing her to feel his big arousal for her.

"Why wait when we can have what we both want right now?" Bakari asked her with a serious yet sexual look in his eyes.

"Right now?" she questioned him back, unsure if this was a good idea or not. "Bakari, that's... crazy."

By now, his hands had landed on the back of her thighs, gently easing them apart before pulling up her dress.

"That is crazy," he agreed with her as he pressed his lips to the back of her ear. "Crazy enough to make you want it right now, right here."

Indira's hands were right by her side, but she suddenly threw her purse to the floor then her hands lifted to his neck, pulling him down so she could join their lips together. While their passionate tongue battle commenced, Bakari quickly pulled down his jeans, followed by his boxers before lifting Indira's thighs to his torso.

Indira internally moaned when she felt the heat of his large bulge directly against her private spot. To feel how turned on he was, was a huge ego boost for her, and at this point, she didn't care about where they were. Nor did she care about them being fully clothed. Nor did she seem to care about protection. It had to be the liquor she'd had earlier and the fact that she was heartbroken by what she had learned about her supposed "fiancé." Bakari Marshall was who she wanted. She wanted this man. Every last inch of him.

Thinking that he was about to pull down her panties, Indira pulled her lips away from his only to look down and push herself slightly away from him. The second she laid eyes on his manhood, she felt faint. *What the...* Javon wasn't even this big, long, *or* thick. He was of average size. A size that she had gotten greatly accustomed to. However, this right here...

Bakari chuckled lightly at her facial expression to his dick, and when she opened her mouth to speak, he pressed his lips against hers once more to shut her up and ease her worries.

"You can... handle it," he whispered between their lips.

"I don't... think I... I ca... ohhhhh!"

While kissing her, Bakari had already pulled her panties to the side and positioned his shaft right by her opening. He slowly pushed into her, only going a couple inches in, and then pulled out. It hurt a little, but with how he was easing in and preparing her for each inch, greatly subsided the pain.

"See? Yes, you can," he told her, sinking his white teeth into his bottom lip as he leaned his hips forward again and penetrated her tight cave. "God damn it..."

He hated how good her pussy felt. He hated it because he now knew that he was in the biggest dilemma of his life. A dilemma that meant that trying to forget about her after this night was going to be impossible.

Indira tightened her grip around his neck and felt him hold her thighs in place around his torso so they wouldn't slip off. Also so she couldn't run away, and then seconds later, *it* truly began.

"Agh... Bakari!"

It being the most intoxicating sex of Indira's entire life.

Every stroke inside her made her feel like she was in a different world. A world that had nothing but feelings of ecstasy. Everlasting ecstasy. Ecstasy that was only becoming more addictive as he moved in and out of her.

"Shit..." It didn't even feel real at first to her. It felt too good to be real. To have a dick like this moving so effortlessly inside her was beyond her wildest dreams. He was fucking her like he had known her for years. Like he was familiar with her tight walls and muscles. Knowing exactly what pace and pattern to fuck her in. Bakari's penetrations gradually increased in momentum, and by now, he was providing her with much more powerful strokes.

"Oh my... God," Indira moaned when he was waist deep inside her guts. To know that basically every inch of him was now inside her tightness only made her wetter for him.

"That's not my name, Indira," he voiced with a smirk and rested his head in the curve of her neck. His heavy breathing filled her ear drums, and both their hearts raced with intense pleasure and adrenaline. The wet, squishy sounds of his dick pounding in and out of her pussy was heard, and Indira couldn't believe how moist she was. Getting this wet never happened to her during sex.

"Remember all that shit you was talking earlier? About having a fiancé like I give a fuck?"

Indira couldn't believe he was bringing up Javon at a time like this. A time that he was thrusting deeper and deeper into her pussy. Who the fuck was Javon anyway? Indira couldn't even give a shit about him. All she cared about was this moment with Bakari. This moment that she never wanted to end.

"Remember?"

"Uhhhh, no," she lied with cries of passion.

"Well I'm 'bout to remind you... remind you that he won't ever be able to fuck you this good," he explained with a deep groan. "He won't ever be able to make you this wet... he won't ever be able to make you cum as hard as I'm going to make you."

His veiny shaft moving along her walls was a feeling like no other. And the fast rhythm at which he was fucking her in meant that the feeling only got worse. Her eyes tightly shut as the sensations of his length moving inside her only got stronger.

"Look at me." His demand immediately made her obey and stare at him. "Keep those eyes fuckin' open. I want to see every last bit of how this dick makes you feel."

Feeling her creaming all over him only made him move at a quicker speed and fill her with more determination. He was determined to get a rise out of her and determined to make her burst first.

"Agh, right there... right there," Indira whimpered, her nails now digging and scratching into his back through his t-shirt.

"Right there?" Bakari teased as he pushed his entire thickness past her folds, smiling as her lips parted, but no words came out. Instead, all that followed were her loud moans and cries. He adjusted his hands to rest on her waist, pumping himself harder between her legs, only heightening her cries of pleasure.

"Yeah, right there," he whispered, knowing he had hit her G-spot. "Right fuckin' there."

"Agh! Ba... Bakari, pul... pull out."

His face instantly scrunched up at her words. *Pull out?* How could he do that when her warm pussy hugged cozily around his dick like a glove. Pulling out was the last thing he could do right now. Fuck it. They were starting a family now.

"It's too... too much," she added with a deep sigh.

"Well you know exactly what to do," he told her. "Cum all over this dick." Indira's heart rate only increased as she listened to his words. "Cum on my dick," he ordered before slowly trailing kisses down her neck and still plunging into her. Her tight walls were only clenching more and more around his rod, so he knew she was close. But he needed her to hurry up because he was extremely close.

He suddenly let go of the side of her waist to reach up to grab her throat. The second he choked and whispered into her ear, "Did I fuckin' stutter, Indira? Cum on my dick right now," she was a goner. "Je ne vais pas vous le dire à nouveau *(I'm not about to tell you again)*."

And then he added what sounded like Haitian French, and Indira was completely done. She may not have understood a word he'd just said, but the shit sounded sexy as fuck and had her gushing like a water faucet. Her whole body began to twitch and shake against him, and then her juices came cascading around his dick just like he had wanted. Knowing that she was submissive to his every word made her realize that she was in trouble.

Big trouble.

Chapter Seven

Indira's eyes slowly fluttered open only for her to see a white door across the room from her. The white door of the hotel bedroom she had checked into last night. The second she tried to move her legs under the sheets, she was immediately reminded of what had gone down last night.

Last night...

Fucking Bakari Marshall had been completely unexpected. If someone had told her at the beginning of this week that she would be in the salon while intruders vandalized it, she would receive head from a stranger, her wedding would be called off, and she would fuck the stranger who had given her head, she never would have believed it.

God, what have I done?

A deep sigh left her lips as she contemplated the predicament she was in. To make things worse, she wasn't supposed to be alone this morning. After fucking her brains out on the balcony, Bakari told her to meet him downstairs, outside in ten minutes. She assumed that he wanted to take her home, but not to her home, to his. And she was all for it because she was still extremely high off their sex. However, when she went into the restrooms to freshen up, looking into her reflection made her feel like a hoe. Her makeup had sweated and smudged in numerous places. She felt embarrassed. The sex may have been spectacular, but she felt used. So she called an Uber, crept out the tattoo shop through the back exit downstairs, and checked into a hotel. She texted Tokyo, letting her know that she had headed home and apologized for not saying goodbye before switching off her phone and falling into a long-needed slumber.

Now here she was, laying in the bed and thinking about all the tribulations of her life. What had seemed like a picture-perfect life was anything but that. Her boyfriend had cheated on her for God knows how long, and now she had done the same to him.

Indira didn't know what to do with herself right now. She was just grateful that today was a Saturday which meant that she could relax without having to worry about work. But one person she knew she was going to have to worry about was... Javon.

After all this time, he still had been cheating on her, and to finally realize that she had been played hurt Indira beyond anything in the whole entire world. This was the man that she basically gave her everything to. Anything he ever needed in this life, without a doubt, she provided it to him without even thinking about the consequences.

I just bought this mothafucka a car, she mused, remembering her act of a few days ago. The act that she had done out of guilt for allowing Bakari to do what he had done that night in the salon. Out of the guilt and love she had for Javon, she wanted to somehow make up for her infidelity. But here she was being the bigger fool this entire time. *I need to return that shit. Ain't no way I'm about to let this nigga drive my car around to go fuck bitches.*

The thought of Javon taking her car around Atlanta to different women's houses, just so they could have sex, disgusted her. That car was expensive, and she was about to get every last penny back.

It took Indira a total of thirty minutes to get cleaned up and dressed into last night's clothing. The fact that she didn't have new clothing to change into made her feel like even more of a hoe. *It's a good thing that you got a hotel instead of following... him.*

Indira had mixed feelings about last night. Undeniably, she had enjoyed the session that her and Bakari shared. It was mind blowing, and the thrill of having sex outside, knowing that they could have been caught at any time, only gassed her further. But what was it all for?

They'd had sex, and both released long time feelings that they'd had for each other. However, what was to become of them now?

Indira didn't see herself getting into a relationship with Bakari Marshall. She was still engaged to another man, and after today, she was sure that she would be done with relationships for a while... right? Bakari didn't seem like a relationship person anyway. She had never seen him with a girl on his arm. So having a relationship with him was highly unlikely.

Twenty minutes later, and the Uber that Indira had requested from her hotel had dropped her right outside her front door. Staring at it only made Indira surer about what she was going to do today. She'd had the entire night to carefully contemplate her decision, and she was sure that it was what needed to be done.

"Baby! Where the hell have you been?"

Once he heard the opening of the front door, Javon was quick on his heels out of his bedroom and straight to the living room.

"I've been calling and text—"

"I switched off my phone," she interrupted him, not bothering to look him in the eye and taking a seat on the nearest beige couch.

From her unbothered tone and the way she refused to look his way, Javon automatically knew something was wrong. So instead of bombarding her with questions that he desperately wanted answers to, he decided to be nicer to her.

"Indi, baby," he gently called out to her as he sauntered toward where she sat and plopped himself down next to her. The minute he tried to hold her, she flinched away from him.

"Don't you dare touch me," she snapped, looking straight ahead at the plasma TV mounted on the ivory wall.

"Indi? What's wrong?"

She took a soft sigh before reaching into her silver purse and pulling out her ring. Javon watched with a perplexed expression as she set it on the coffee table ahead and turned to look at him.

"I want the key to the coupe I bought you."

"W-What? Why?"

"I want the key you own that allows you to get into this house," she added, ignoring his questions. "And I want you to get your shit and get the fuck out of my house."

"Indira... what the hell are you talking about?"

"I know!" she yelled as her eyes welled up with tears when she turned to face him. "I know all about what you've been doing behind my back!"

"Indira, I don't know what you're talking about. Baby, I haven't been doing anything."

"Don't you dare lie to me," Indira retorted, pushing his hands away when he tried to reach out to her again. "You've been lying to me for months. The least you owe me right now is the truth!"

"And what truth is that?" he asked her with a dumbfounded look.

"The bitch that texted you a few days ago? Well guess where I met her? At the party my boss invited me to. And I heard all about your little coaching situation, you idiot!" Indira immediately lifted her fist to hit him only to be stopped by his grip. "I hate you so much! I fucking hate you! Let go of me!"

"Indira, stop tryna hit me! I don't know what the fuck you're talking about! Indira, stop!" he shouted, still fighting to keep her fists away from him. "Indira, for fuck's sake, I haven't cheated on you! Why the fuck are you acting like this?"

"You've been messing around on me for months, with that girl and God knows who!" She cried, releasing her fists out his grip and getting up from the couch. "I want you out! Right now!"

Javon started to fill with anger at Indira's attitude toward him.

"I'm not going anywhere because I haven't done anything wrong! You claim I'm cheating on you, but with who? Who the fuck am I gonna cheat with?" he asked as she began pacing up and down the room.

"That bitch that texted you about sitting on your face," she retorted, her face scrunched up with fury and a few tears already dropping out of her eyes.

"The one that was a wrong number? Indi, baby, we both saw those messages, and you know I didn't know who that was."

"Well you're a damn liar, because she was in the restroom when I was in the restroom, and I heard her reveal about you coaching her to pretend like she doesn't know you," Indira explained as she halted in her place and then pointed at him. "You've been lying to me, and unless you get the fuck out of my house in the next ten minutes, you're going to make me do something that I'll most likely regret."

"Oh, so you're threatening me now?" Javon asked her incredulously. "You're threatening your fiancé now, Indi? Okay, since you don't believe me, how about we call this girl that I've apparently been cheating on you with?"

"Fine by me," Indira answered, crossing her arms against her chest. "You even have her number which means you definitely know her."

"No, I still have her number because I forgot to delete those messages from a few days ago. I've been taking care of my sick father, in case you magically forgot," he snapped at her before sighing deeply. "Let me call her and make you see that I don't know her at all."

Indira gave him a suspicious look before stiffly nodding for him to make the call. She knew that the call wasn't going to change anything at all because she knew that he was cheating on her. That girl in the bathroom had a story too similar to the one that she had experienced. He was cheating on her, and that was it.

While Indira stayed standing, Javon whipped out his phone from his back pocket, dialing the number and placing his phone on speaker phone.

"Hello?"

A female voice came on the line and Indira observed Javon carefully.

"Hi," he greeted her friendly. "I'm the guy that you accidentally texted a few days back."

"Oh yeah! So sorry about that."

"It's okay. Could you please just convince my girl that you don't know me? She believes I'm cheating on her for some dumb reason. I have you on loud speaker by the way."

"Oh no, honey. I seriously texted the wrong number. I was trying to message my ex-boyfriend but got a few numbers wrong when I was trying to remember it by heart. Trust me, I don't know your man."

And just to confirm, you weren't at a party yesterday talking about being coached by a taken man?" Javon asked her.

"A party? Man, I wish. I work late shifts, Monday to Friday at a store. I have no time for parties."

"Thank you so much for the confirmation. Take care," Javon concluded.

"You too."

The call ended, and Javon looked up from his phone only to see Indira's teary eyes.

"See, baby?" he told her as he got up from his seat and dropped his phone on the couch. "I'm not cheating on you with anybody."

Indira's tears started pouring down her cheeks, and when Javon was close enough to pull her into his arms, she only sobbed harder.

"It's okay," he gently cooed into her ears, stroking her back. "You just gotta trust me, Indi. Trust me."

And that was the reason why she was crying. She didn't trust this man one bit. Not one.

"Girl, there's a man here to see you out front. A fine ass man if I might say so myself."

Katrina looked up from her desk and felt a smile form on her lips. She already knew exactly who was here to see her, and her excitement to see him now was uncontrollable. He had come to surprise her at work, and she couldn't wait to see him.

"Thank you for letting me know," she told her colleague, Raven, before getting up from her seat and leaving her desk.

She worked Monday to Friday at a call center, and despite how much she hated her job, it was really all she had. Dropping out of college hadn't been the greatest decision of her life, but she wasn't about to go back on it ever. But moving to Atlanta to be closer to her man was a decision she was willing to make, so she did it.

Katrina headed to the front entrance of her work place with a wide smile on her face. She couldn't wait to see Carl. Not being able to lay eyes on him for a few days had her feeling disheartened, but knowing that he was here to see her now lifted her spirits completely.

However, getting to the front entrance and not seeing Carl anywhere in sight made her fill with confusion.

What the hell? Didn't Raven say he wa—

"You're Carl's girl, right?"

Katrina turned to the side to see an undeniably attractive man walking toward her. He was light skinned, not her usual type, but this man right here was beautiful. Just seeing the way his pink, plump lips moved as he spoke to her made her feel wetness down below. Even as he was walking toward her, he seemed like a tall giant, especially since she was only five two.

"Yes, that's me," she answered him in a friendly tone. "And you are?"

"Have you seen him?" he asked, dismissing her question.

"No," Katrina quietly said, looking up at him and feeling intimidated. "Who are you?"

Again, he ignored her question and towered over her once he was directly in front of her.

"Are you sure you haven't seen him?"

Katrina felt her heart begin to race. With the way this man was staring at her stoically, she only felt more intimidated by him. She shook her head no at him.

"I really hope you're not lying to me right now, Katrina."

What the... How does he know my name? Horror started to build within her heart.

"How do you know my name? Who are you?" she nervously queried.

"I'm the man that's about to become your new biggest mothafuckin' nightmare if you keep lying to me," Bakari warned her with a sexy smile.

How could a man be so fine but so dangerous looking at the same time? This was the kind of man she didn't want to get on the wrong side of.

"I swear I'm not lying," she said in a pleading tone. "I haven't seen Carl for days now."

"But you're his girl," Bakari simply reminded her. "You moved to Atlanta to be closer to him, so how the fuck aren't you seeing him?"

Oh my God. How does he know all of this information about me?

"He's only been texting and calling me. I swear I haven't seen him. I can show you our messages."

"You're going to do something even better for me," Bakari announced. "You're going to let him know that you urgently need to see him, and make sure he meets you at a location I'll tell you to tell him."

Katrina's face instantly twisted into an unsure look.

"I-I can't do that," she shakily answered him. A deadly look instantly formed in his eyes as he gazed down at her.

"It wasn't a request," he told her before stepping closer to her and placing his hand to her right cheek. "You wouldn't want me to start cutting you off piece by piece and mailing you in the post office to your auntie back in Dallas?" Katrina's face went white, and her lower lip trembled as he gently caressed her cheek. "Would you?"

She quickly shook her head no, and that gave Bakari enough confirmation.

"I want you to turn to the left and walk straight ahead to that black Wraith. If you even attempt to run, I promise you that that concrete floor will be the last material you'll ever feel against your skin before a bullet cracks your head wide open. Got it?"

She obediently nodded. Her eyes were now wet, and she was barely able to breathe. His hand stroked her cheek one last time before he removed it. Then he observed as she did as he had ordered and walked toward the Wraith before getting in. A grin graced his lips as his goon in the driver's seat drove off with Carl's girl now in the back seat.

Chapter Eight

Two Days Later

"What's in the bag?"

"What you asked for," Bakari simply stated as he stared at his sister carefully.

Tokyo squinted at him before looking at Yasir who had a small smirk on his face.

"Yasir, what's in the bag?" she asked him, hoping that he would be more open than her brother was.

"Take a look yourself, T," Bakari pressed on. "Why you tryna act brand new? You asked for it."

"Just tell me what's inside," she whined, looking at the black gym bag that sat on her desk.

"Carl's head," Yasir finally spoke up as he leaned back comfortably in his seat. "The main bitch he was cheating on you with is in there too."

"Already?" she asked as she slowly unzipped the bag only to peek through to see the heads of Carl and his girlfriend. The stench of death and decay hit her nostrils, and she immediately shut the bag to mask it. "Well that went quicker than I anticipated."

"Yeah, he tried to skip town, but we got his ass," Yasir explained coolly. "His girl gave him up just fine thanks to Bakari's persuasion. He was so persuasive that she actually thought she was going to live to tell this whole tale," Yasir said with a light chuckle.

"Thank you," Tokyo responded. "Now can you both get this out of here? It reeks."

Yasir simply nodded and got up out of his seat to grab the bag. Bakari then walked away from the blinds and headed toward her desk.

"T, remember what I said," he announced seriously. "Chill on the crazy shit."

"Yeah, yeah, whatever," she said, waving him goodbye as she began clicking away on her MacBook.

The two men made their way out of her office; Yasir remained ahead while Bakari was behind. He gently shut Tokyo's office door behind him. The minute he stepped outside, his eyes wandered down the corridor that led to the work space on the other side. The work space that belonged to the woman that he had been furious with all weekend.

"Yo, Yasir," Bakari called out to him, making Yasir turn around to face him with a curious look. "Go ahead without me. I'll hit you up you later on tonight."

"You sure, B?"

Bakari nodded firmly at him, and Yasir took this as his confirmation to get gone. But he wasn't a fool though. He knew where Bakari was going or in fact who Bakari was going to. He definitely had seen the way Bakari had looked at her nonstop when she first stepped into the tattoo shop party.

"A'ight, see you later then," Yasir concluded before heading through the back door of the salon.

Bakari sauntered toward the white door on the other side of the building and twisted its golden handle without even knocking to let the occupant of the room know that he was outside.

Indira had her back to the door while she opened up a new packet of eyelash extensions, but upon hearing the door open, she turned around with a smile thinking that Tokyo had come to check up on her.

"Hey, T, wha..." Her smile to quickly faded when she laid eyes on that handsome face. Her heart immediately pounded rapidly in her chest as he shut the door behind him.

Oh God.

He looked fine as hell. His clothing for the day was a khaki Nike tracksuit with matching khaki Nike Air Vapormax on his feet. The color khaki complimented his light mocha skin extremely well.

"You left me that night and thought I wouldn't find your ass, huh? Did your ass suddenly get amnesia and forget you work for my sister?" His question had been blunt, but alongside it, he released a light chuckle. A light chuckle that told her he wasn't finding anything funny.

"Bakari, I..."

"You what?" he asked.

"I couldn't... I couldn't go home with you," she admitted truthfully.

"Why not?"

"...Because it's wrong. I'm engaged."

"You being engaged was the last thing on your mind when I was in betw—"

"Bakari, it was a mistake," she interrupted him. "You and I both know that."

His neutral facial expression was gradually turning into irritation. She could see it growing in his eyes the more he watched her. However, instead of saying anything further to her, Bakari left the door and started walking to where she sat on her high chair.

Seeing that he was coming toward her made her develop the urge to want to flee. There was just something about the way that he was looking at her now that told her staying in her seat was a bad idea. But when she finally plucked up the courage to get up, she was too late. He had already made it to her.

"Bakari, I'm so..." She started out her sentence, but when his hand grabbed her throat, she instantly stopped talking. It wasn't the grab of her throat that made her stop talking. It was the pool she could now feel forming in her panties as he held her throat.

"Interrupt me again," he whispered into her left ear. "And I'll fuck you and that pussy up. Right here, right now." Indira felt her insides fire up at his warning. "Now what were you saying? You're what?" he questioned her curiously, tightening his grip around her throat slightly.

"I'm sorry," she whispered, trying to stop herself from getting wet down below. But there was no use. One of her weaknesses was being choked, and the night they'd had sex together, he had worked it out. Now he was using it to his advantage.

"Yeah, you should be sorry," he told her coolly. "You left me that night with no warning, no goodbye, and no kiss. I searched that whole entire shop for you, even going into the girls' restroom. Why did you leave?"

"I told you, Bakari. What we did was a mistake. I'm engaged," she said in a low tone.

"And I don't really give a fuck," Bakari affirmed while leaning in closer to her with his hand still wrapped around her throat. "It changes nothing."

She gave him an absurd look before responding, "It changes everything."

"No it doesn't."

"Yes it does."

"So you're arguing with me now?" he questioned her with a deadly look in his eyes. Indira remained silent and just looked at him with an intrigued look. "You're arguing with me now?" he repeated, tightening his hand around her neck and pushing her head back.

The smile that crept on her face was one that she couldn't help at all. Bakari knew she liked being choked, so this wasn't hurting her one bit. Only turning her on. But seeing that she wasn't taking him seriously made him loosen his grip around her and back away from her with a frown.

"Your freaky ass ain't even paying attention to me," he informed her with a head shake.

"Bakari, what do you want from me?" she suddenly asked, staring closely at him. His facial expression began to soften, but he was yet to open his mouth and answer her query. So that encouraged her to speak further. "We had sex, yeah, you gave me head, but what now? You've gotten what you wanted, and I told you it was a mistake, so why are you here? What do you still want from me?"

Bakari stayed standing stoically in his stance as he listened to her questions. He could see the mixture of intrigue and confusion in her eyes. On one hand, she was intrigued by him and all the pleasure he had to offer her, but on the other hand, she was confused by him.

"What do I want from you?" he asked her quietly as he started walking back toward her. "You know exactly what I want, Indira." Once in front of her seat, he grabbed her waist and looked down at her without breaking eye contact. "I want you. I want her," he said, his eyes drifting down momentarily to her inner thighs before snapping back up to her eyes again. "Wherever and however I want her. And I'm here to let you know that that little stunt you pulled last week won't ever happen again. I want all of you and intend to have you. You can sit here and pretend like you don't want me too, but it's bullshit. We both know it. Your fiancé doesn't matter, Indira. The sooner you realize that, the better."

Without even giving her the chance to respond, Bakari branded their lips together and began to tongue her down passionately. Their wet flesh entwined perfectly, and Indira was unable to stop herself from getting lost in his lips. He was such a good, dominant kisser, and she was unable to resist it.

When his lips pulled away from hers and started kissing down her neck, Indira softly sighed and placed her hands around him, pulling him closer. She'd caught a whiff of his attractive aroma when he first walked over to her, but now that he was directly next to her, she was drowning in it. And she'd never wanted to drown as bad as she was now.

"Bakari... not here... I'm still working," she whispered, biting her lips because of how much his neck kisses were turning her on.

"When... do you... get off?" he queried between his seductive pecks.

"After my... next client. For lunch."

He said nothing in return and gave the curve of her neck a few more kisses before coming up from her neck.

"Nah, when do you get off finally for the day?"

"My last appointment finishes at around eight," she explained.

"I'll come get you then," he stated simply before letting go of her waist and deciding it was time to go.

Seeing him start to walk away from her made her heart drop a little, but it quickly recovered when she remembered he was coming back for her. He sauntered toward the door, and once by it, he pulled for the handle before turning back around to see her pretty face staring at him.

"If you run away like you did last time, I promise you that you will regret it," he warned lightly. "I still haven't forgotten you running away, and trust me, I don't intend to let that shit slide, Indira. At all."

She continued to stare at him, fright filling her but also excitement. He then turned away from her, pulled open the door, and left, leaving Indira to deeply think about what had just gone down in the last ten minutes.

I can't believe this is happening... She truly couldn't. All weekend, she'd tried to push her feelings away for that man out the window. She even believed that when she took her morning after pill that it would not just rid her of her chance to get pregnant, but also her feelings about Bakari. However, it had done no such thing. And of course it didn't help that she was no longer trusting of Javon. He may have gotten the girl who accidentally texted him to confirm that they didn't know each other, but Indira still didn't trust him. At this point, all she wanted was some space, and since he wasn't home Monday through Friday, she would have all the space she required. Although now it seemed like she would be using that space to spend time with Bakari Marshall.

"Arjana."

Arjana refused to look up from her drawing to see who had just stepped into her open booth. She knew who it was, and quite frankly didn't want to see his annoying, sexy face.

"Can I see you in my office, please?"

"Why?" she asked back, not in the mood to talk to him.

"This ain't a debate," he fumed. "My office. Now." Then he left the doorway of her booth and headed to his office.

Arjana immediately rolled her eyes at him before catching the glance of Allison, her assistant, who had a cheeky grin on her lips.

"Someone's in troubleeee," Allison sang as Arjana got up from her seat.

"I haven't done shit to him," Arjana voiced with dismay while walking toward the exit.

"Well, I'll be praying for you, girl," Allison joked.

Arjana made her way to his office on the second floor and sighed deeply when she saw him standing in the doorway waiting for her.

"Close the door," he ordered as he walked inside.

Arjana entered and shut the door behind her as he wanted. The second the door shut, he was onto her like a cheetah racing to its prey. She didn't even have a chance to say anything because he grabbed her arm and pulled her into his embrace before locking lips with her.

"Ya... Ya... sir."

His lips meshed with hers, controlling the start of a fiery battle, and his hands landed on her butt through her jeans, squeezing tightly and caressing her cheeks like she was a genie that needed to grant him three wishes. It seemed like no matter how hard she tried to keep things professional between them, he was always adamant on taking it that one step further. He was supposed to be her boss, but here he was, using his power to lure her into his office and tongue her down.

"Ya... sir, stop," she said once breaking her lips away from his.

Looking up into his hooded mahogany eyes made her wish that she hadn't. He was so fine that it was annoying to her.

His smooth chocolate skin was something that she'd found attractive from the second she laid eyes on him. There was just something about a nigga with chocolate skin that had always made her melt inside with pure happiness. On his low-cut head were waves, his face housed a full beard, and around his pink, plump lips sat a thick moustache. It was no surprise to see a flesh full of tattoos peeking from under his black t-shirt. He owned a tattoo shop and was considered one of the best tattoo artists in Georgia, so it was only fitting that he had tattoos all over his body. Yasir towered over her at six one with a powerful physique; his muscles were the perfect size, not too large, and not too small. To put it simple, he was sexy.

"What, baby?"

"Why do you keep doing this shit? You know I want us to just work together professionally."

Yasir internally sighed as he looked down at her. For someone so gorgeous, she truly knew how to dampen his mood. From the second he laid eyes on her, he knew that this was the woman that he wanted to spend the rest of his life with. Arjana was half African-American and half Filipino. Her mix of African-American and Filipino gave her small, jewel-like green eyes. She had perfectly arched brows which sat on her silken cinnamon skin and a long, well sculpted nose. Her glossy lips were full and delicate, his favorite feature on her after her eyes. Arjana's coffee brown hair was long and straight, reaching the bottom of her back. Standing at five seven, she had a slim body with hips, small breasts, and a little booty that Yasir loved to palm all the time. Her booty may have been small, but the way he made her feel was like she had the best booty in the world.

"And I hear you on that, but I also want us to work together in other ways," he commented with a smirk as he squeezed her ass.

"Yasir, we broke up," she reminded him.

"Because of you," he reminded her. "I told you I didn't want to end things, but you said you didn't want to be in a relationship."

"And I still don't want to be."

"So why were you in my bed last night?" he asked her cockily. "Huh?"

She rolled her eyes at him and attempted to leave his embrace.

"No. Answer the question, Arjana," he demanded, spanking her hard. "Why were you in a nigga's bed last night, the night before that, and the night before that?"

Arjana refused to answer and just gave him a nasty stare, hating herself for enjoying the hard slap he had delivered on her butt.

"Cat got your tongue?"

"Shut up," she told him rudely.

"Make me," he challenged her with a grin before placing his lips on her neck. "Make me shut up, Arjana," he seductively taunted her.

As much as she hated how much he knew how to get her to succumb to him, she also loved it. Their relationship may have been complicated, but because their sex was amazing, it made their complicated situation worth it.

She placed her hands in the small gap between them before sitting them on his bulge. Yasir's eyes started widening when he felt her hand beginning to stroke his erection through his pants. Seeing the lust growing in his eyes only encouraged her to keep rubbing him quicker, and with each motion, his erection grew. The second he felt himself wanting to groan, he slapped her hands away and grabbed her waist.

Arjana gasped when he lifted her up to his torso and began walking them over to his desk. Without hesitating, he cleared his entire desk, sending everything to the floor, and setting her on top of it. Then their lips locked back to each other's, and they frantically began stripping each other's clothing off.

The desire to have Yasir had completely overtaken her stubborn nature to keep things professional between them. She truly couldn't help herself around him. One minute, she wanted to be far away from him, and then the next, she was all he wanted. He was the dangerous drug that she couldn't stop taking. The aphrodisiac she never wanted to stop having.

Chapter Nine

"Oh my... Oh my God!"

"What'd I tell you about that shit, huh? What'd I... ah, fuck! What'd I say? That's not my name. Say my name," he demanded as he quickly pushed in and out of her tight slit. He lifted a hand to her throat and squeezed tightly on her flesh. "Say my fuckin' name."

His thickness moved in and out of her in a steady, quick fashion. Her sensuous moans filled the room accompanied by his groans and the king-sized bed shaking noisily.

"Bakar... Mr. Marshall," she corrected herself, knowing it would only drive him crazy.

"Shit, Indira... don't call me that," he voiced as he pulled out before pushing back into her.

On the drive to his home, Bakari had taken a call through his car phone unit, and it had turned out to be a business associate. The associate had started the call with, "Mr. Marshall?" And for some odd reason, Indira really liked hearing the professional manner that Bakari was being addressed in. She had called him it at the start of their sex session unknowingly, and the look of lust that formed on his face only told her one thing: he loved her calling him that.

"Uhh... Why not, Mr. Marshall?" she breathlessly asked. "You, ugh!... You want me to call you by your name, right?"

"You little tease," he whispered to her as he pounded harder inside her. Looking down only to see her wrists constantly shaking behind her made him smile to himself. "Stop tryna run, Indira," he instructed her, moving his hand from her throat and holding her wrists down. "You can't anyways. Not with these bad boys on you."

"Ahhh! Bakari!"

Each time he slipped his hard length inside her, Indira felt overwhelmed. Overwhelmed at how good and bad it all felt. His hips only thrusted against her ass cheeks quicker as he fucked her pussy from the back. Beads of sweat had broken out all over her naked body, and her thighs were getting damper by the second. Then she felt his tongue lick and suck on her upper back until his lips landed on the curve of her neck. Her mind spun with lust and love for how affectionate and aggressive he was being.

"Putain, j'adore ta chatte (*Fuck, I love your pussy*)." He whispered French into her ear, which only turned her on further. The fact that he was fluent in both Haitian Creole and French was something that she loved. Hearing him throw in the sexiest phrases in his native tongue while he fucked her was becoming one of the best things in her life.

Wrist restraints were currently on her wrists, courtesy of him. He hadn't been joking earlier when he said he wasn't going to let her suddenly leaving him last week slide. Black leather wrist restraints were clasped tightly on her wrists while her arms were behind her.

This was the second time that he had tied her hands away. Only this time, he had the proper equipment and not just her simple hair tie. Being tied up was a first for Indira, and as dirty as it made her feel, she loved it. She loved knowing that he had restricted her movement so she couldn't run from his drilling. She loved feeling like a bad woman that needed to be locked up by him and punished. He was bringing out sides of her that she didn't even know truly existed. Introducing her to a side of him that she never would have guessed he had.

Bakari seemed quiet and reserved at first glance. But the truth was that this man was a freak. An absolute freak that knew how to please her in every single spot on her body. His speed only increased, and with each fuck, Indira could feel herself getting closer to the edge. His pumps were breathtaking—literally—because Indira barely could breathe. The way he filled her up so full and snug was taking away her breath. And he had a technique of thrusting into her and then keeping himself inside her for a few seconds to rotate his hips. When she felt his dick moving in a circle inside her, she truly lost it.

As soon as her climax coated his shaft, he quickly pulled out of her so that he wouldn't release his load inside her. He had a much better plan in store than to do that.

After letting her recover from her high, Bakari requested for her to get on her knees on his bedroom floor, and what he did next was unexpected but strangely gratifying to Indira. He looked down at her with awe as she smiled when his nut came shooting at her and landed on her pretty face.

"Look at you," he announced with a groan. "Enjoying this shit. You like me cumming on your face?"

She obediently nodded, sticking out her tongue to sexily lick the traces of his climax that had landed near her mouth.

"I love it," she innocently admitted.

"You little, nasty bitch," he whispered.

"Mr. Marshall's little, nasty bitch," she corrected him, and it only made him grin wide at her. He then observed as she moved closer between his thighs before lifting his manhood into her mouth and sucking off the remaining traces of his climax. "Shit... Indira."

Twenty minutes later, the pair of them had showered and were now lying in bed together, facing each other. He had his arms wrapped around her to keep her as close to him as possible, and smelling her sweet scent was driving him crazy.

"I've never let a man do that to me before." Her announcement made him gaze deeper into her pupils.

"What, tie you up and shit?"

"That too... but nut on me," she revealed. "You do that often?"

"Yeah," he coolly said, watching the surprise that formed in her eyes. "No."

She gave him an unconvinced look, so he decided to keep talking.

"Yeah, I've done it before, but not in a while. Same with the tying up stuff. I don't just do that to anyone. It takes real effort to want to please someone beyond just having consensual sex. With you... shit just feels different."

A small smile grew on her lips before responding, "I mean, I feel nasty but good nasty, I guess. You're lucky I like you to even let you restrain me in the first place."

"So you like me, huh?" he questioned her cockily.

Indira said nothing and decided to look down at his naked, muscular chest. Just like how she pictured him to look under his clothes, he looked and even better. Her chin was quickly lifted up, so she was forced to look back into his striking brown irises.

"You like me," he happily announced with a grin, flashing his whites at her.

"I guess I do," she said simply. "Do you like me?"

"I wouldn't nut all over your pretty face if I didn't, sweetheart," he replied with a chuckle which made her playfully roll her eyes at him. "Are you hungry?"

She nodded at him. After their heated back to back sessions for the past few hours, she had worked up a strong appetite.

Bakari's home was in the outskirts of Atlanta, in Alpharetta, one of the richest cities in Georgia. It was a four-bedroom home sitting on a very private heavily wooded one-acre lot. The driveway was attractive and long which made Indira feel like she was entering a new, private world when he pulled up to his home. It had a total of three bathrooms, an attached parking garage, where he had stored his alluring Aston Martin. His home had a masculine yet neutral feel to it. The colors ivory, white, black, beige, and mahogany were the main colors of his humble abode.

Sitting opposite him on his dining table made her feel quite nervous. Especially because she was about to try some of his cooking. However, once lifting the Haitian dish to her lips and taking a taste, it turned out to be delicious. *So he can fuck me right, and he's a good cook?* she mused to herself as she kept eating. *What can't he do right?*

"You like it?"

His question made her look up from her plate of food and smile at him pleasantly. She nodded, swallowing her bites before speaking up.

"It's delicious. Thank you. What is it though? I taste chicken and see beans..."

"It's Mayi Moulen ak Sòs Pwa, Poul an Sòs," he spoke in his native tongue and laughed at the confusion forming on her pretty face. "Cornmeal with beans and stewed chicken," he translated for her, putting her out of her misery.

"It's so good." She complimented his food while taking more bites.

Bakari said nothing in response and kept on eating while watching her closely. Feeling his gaze on her as she continued to eat made her feel shy once again. Her eyes drifted back up at him, and she gave him a curious look. A curious look that he could read instantly.

"What, so I can't look at you?" he asked as he dropped his fork. She noticed the way his tongue slipped out of his mouth and wet his bottom lip.

Indira immediately began to blush at his question and attempted to look away from him once again until he spoke up again.

"Me looking at you whenever I want and how I want is something that you're going to have to get used to," he stated confidently. "Especially when you have a face and body like that."

"Well you better get used to me looking at you just as hard," she said boldly.

"Oh really?" One of his brows raised. "And why's that?"

"You know why."

"Nah, I don't. Enlighten me."

Indira instantly began to beam when she realized what he was trying to get her to admit to him right now.

"You do... You know how sexy you are, Bakari," she told him while biting her lips at him. Just staring into his brown eyes was making her desire for him heighten.

Seeing her bite her lips at him was sending him back into a mood that wasn't appropriate right now, especially since they were eating.

"Eat your food, Indira," he ordered while picking up his fork, "before you start some shit you can't handle."

Fighting off the urge to find out the deeper meaning behind his words and show him exactly what she could handle, Indira kept on eating the remaining pieces of her meal.

"Who taught you how to cook?" she asked him curiously, wanting to know where he had picked up his talent from.

"Both my mom and dad," he voiced. "But mostly my Haitian father."

"So your father taught you how to cook Haitian dishes?"

"Yup," he said coolly. "He's the pro, so I learnt from the best."

"This was really good though... I wonder what else you can cook."

"Well you'll just have to wait and see," he seductively informed her. "Can you cook?"

"No... well... kinda," she shyly stated, knowing she wasn't the best cook, but she did what she could. "I try, but I can't cook as well as this."

"You should learn. Cooking is a great skill to have."

"You gonna teach me?"

He gave her an interested look before responding with, "You want to learn from me?"

"Maybe," she innocently stated. "You don't want to teach me?"

"Who said that?" he queried. "I'm down to teach you how to cook and teach you how to do... other things."

The sexual tone that appeared in his voice made her throw him a sexy smile.

"Sounds like a plan."

It was only a few minutes later when Indira was greeted to her phone screen brightening up, alerting her of an incoming email. It made her notice the time which was now 11:30 p.m.

Damn, it's that late already? I need to get going. I have work in the morning.

"You gotta go?"

His question made her look up from her phone only to see the blank expression on his handsome face.

"Yeah," she confirmed. "Work tomorrow, so I need to go over all my bookings."

"No worries. I'll take you back myself."

"No, Bakari. I can just take an Uber," she insisted, but her words went in one ear and out the other.

"Let me know when you're ready to go," he stated coolly.

The drive home was quiet. To get back to Atlanta from Alpharetta was thirty minutes. He didn't say a word, and neither did she. A small part of her felt awkward because they'd had sex for the last couple hours, and now he was taking her home. She looked out the window and admired the night view of the city.

"I'm coming back for you tomorrow."

His announcement made her whip her head around to observe him. He had his eyes on the road ahead, but momentarily, he gave her a glance and then focused ahead once again.

"And the day after tomorrow, the day after that, and the day after that," he added. "I want you in my bed for the rest of this week."

"...I can't, Bakari... I have my god sister coming in tomorrow, and she's not familiar with the city. I gotta take care of her and show her around."

"That ain't got shit to do with you being in my bed, Indira," he told her simply as he took a sharp left.

"It does, because I need to work this week, finish work, then go home, change, then meet up with her. By the time we finish, it'll be late, which means I'll need to sleep so I can wake up on time for work."

Bakari remained silent, contemplating her words for a few seconds before responding. "How long is your god sister in town for?"

"Just a few days," Indira said. "She leaves on Saturday."

"So I gotta wait four days without getting a taste of you again? Fuck..."

Indira couldn't help but smile to herself when she could hear the annoyance in his voice. Having to go four days without her was something he clearly didn't want to do.

"As soon as she's on a flight, you call me."

"Yes," she promised, unable to stop her growing smile.

"Not a second later, Indira."

"Yes." She laughed, and it made him turn to look at her, only to see her smile.

"You're loving this," he commented. "Look at you gassed and shit."

She simply shrugged and smiled harder as she watched him drive.

"I'm serious though, Indira... Not a second later."

"Got it, Mr. Marshall."

He flashed her a sexual look before focusing back on his driving. It was only a few minutes later when he pulled up in front of her home.

"Pass me your phone," he instructed, and Indira grabbed her phone out of her front pocket. She unlocked it before passing it to him.

Bakari's fingers tapped on her bright screen for a few seconds as he placed his number in her phone. Then he passed her phone back to her. Instead of actually giving it to her, when her hand came near, he reached for her wrist and gently pulled her out her seat, toward him. When she was close enough, he branded their lips together and kissed her sensually.

"Call... me," he said in between his sweet pecks on her lips.

She obediently nodded and gave him one last peck before taking her phone from him, turning around to take her leave. The only problem was as soon as she turned away from him, her arm was pulled so that she was facing him again. His lips landed back on hers, and their romantic kiss commenced once again.

When he ended the kiss, their foreheads touched, and their eyes opened to connect with one another. He didn't even have to say it. She could see it in his eyes that he didn't want her to go anywhere. And quite frankly, she didn't want to go anywhere either.

"I'll call you. I promise," she concluded before giving him one last peck. Then he finally let her go to head to her door.

Once in her home, she released a deep exhale when she realized what a day she'd had. She still couldn't really believe what had gone down today with Bakari. Erotic images of him fucking her flashed into her mind, and all she could think about was him.

Indira got ready for bed with a never-ending smile on her face. Being alone and free to think about Bakari without any worries, greatly eased her mind. But as quickly as the ease came, guilt flashed into her mind. Guilt at what she was doing when she knew she was engaged. She eventually managed to push it to the back of her mind and fell asleep. Thinking about when she would next lay eyes on Bakari was what she dreamt about. However, three hours later, her slumber was cut short from the loud ringing of the front doorbell.

Ding Dong!

It made her wake up instantly, and she rubbed her eyes tiredly to relieve her blurry eyes. She reluctantly got out of bed to see who was at the door only to frown when she spotted the sleeping face of Noah and her mother who was holding him.

"Mom, what's going on?"

As soon as she opened the door, the teary eyes of her mother was revealed to her.

"Indi... baby," her mom greeted her in a disheartened tone. "Your brother and I have been evicted. We have nowhere else to go, baby. Please... can we stay with you?"

Chapter Ten

Tokyo grinned happily as she walked around the shop floor, impressed at what she could see. Everyone was hard at work, pleasing clients, and bringing in cash. Just three of the main things she loved to see. Nothing made her happier than her salon, and seeing it grow each day with more clients was an incredible feeling.

Her salon was something that she had put her blood, sweat, and tears into. Seeing it only get more popular was something she adored. All the time she got questions on if she would expand soon and open a new store, but for Tokyo, the answer right now was no. She wanted to remain focused on this branch for a few more years, then soon after, she would consider opening a new store somewhere else in Atlanta.

"That braiding pattern is everything, girl," Tokyo complimented one of her hairstylists who was currently installing a braided ponytail for a client.

"Thank you, T. I wanted to try something different."

"Well keep it up, girl. That looks too bomb," she concluded, about to head back into her office to check some emails, when the opening of the front door sounded.

Tokyo's head snapped in the direction of the door. She thought a client had entered, but seeing an attractive male face come through the door changed her thoughts completely. He had AirPods plugged into both ears, and once stepping in, he let one out.

"Can I help you?" Shea, the receptionist by the front door, asked him in a friendly tone.

Her question made him momentarily break eye contact with Tokyo to look at her.

"I'm here to get my hair cut," he announced confidently. The confident tone that he had spoken up in made every single hairstylist and nail technician remain silent and closely look at him.

It wasn't usual for a male to step into Tokyo's Slay Spot unless they were homosexual and here for an appointment or just here to pick up their girlfriend, sister, mother, or daughter. It was a female dominated salon, because the target audience was females. However, it wasn't a crime for a man to want to get his hair cut in a female salon. Besides, Tokyo's barber was more than ready to give him exactly what he needed and more.

"Great. Well just take a seat, and our female barber will call you over shortly."

"Can you cut my hair?"

Failing to read the fact that his eyes had drifted away from her, Shea thought that he was talking to her.

"Who, me?" she asked in an overly flattered tone.

"Nah, not you." He dismissed her without taking his eyes off Tokyo. "You."

Tokyo at first was bewildered by his constant stare. But now that he was talking directly to her, she realized that he wanted her doing his hair.

"I can't cut hair," she explained simply. "But I assure you that my barber is the best and will give you a good haircut."

"Damn," he said with disappointment. "I wanted your hands on my head."

A small smirk grew on Tokyo's lips, and when she took a glance at her hairstylists and nail techs, she could see their widening eyes and amused expressions.

"And why's that?" she questioned him, intrigued by the small flirting he had started between them in front of everyone.

"'Cause you look like you have a special touch," he responded, flashing a toothy smile her way. "A very special touch."

"And you know this how?" she continued to question him, folding her arms across her chest.

"With a face as gorgeous as that, how could you not have a special touch?" he inquired genuinely.

Damn it. This sexy stranger knows just what to say and how to say it, she mused.

And she was right. This sexy stranger was able to say just the right words to have her secretly swooning over him. The same way that all the workers were swooning over him. How could they not? Not only was he tall, his handsome, oval face was flawless. He had a full, low cut beard along his jawline, a moustache around his shapely pink lips, and healthy, thick brows. His eyes were hooded and the darkest brown that Tokyo had ever seen in her life. His overgrown hair sat on the top of his head in a low afro, framing and suiting his face well. Under the denim shirt he was wearing, his arms filled out the sleeves lovingly. Yeah, he was a beautiful man indeed.

"But since you can't cut hair, I guess I'll just take the next best option," he said, giving her one last glance before taking his seat in the waiting area. Tokyo watched him for a few seconds before snapping out of her trance and heading straight to her office.

As fine as he was, the one thing she wasn't about to do was left him ruin her celibacy life. She had been on a roll and hadn't fallen into the temptations of a man. And that's the way she wanted things to remain.

"I can't believe she's doing it again, and you're allowing her to!"

"Emaza, what am I supposed to do? That's my mother," Indira responded with a deep sigh. "I can't abandon her."

"She's abandoned you so many times before, Indi," Emaza

reminded her. "You know she's just looking for a place to stay, and as soon as she's found her rich baller, she's outta there."

Indira sighed once again before lifting her strawberry daiquiri to her lips and taking a sip. It was good to be able to spend some time with her god sister this evening. They were currently at a local bar downtown because Emaza wanted some liquor in her system ASAP. Her exact words.

Having a god sister was a true godsend for Indira, and her father choosing Emaza as her god sister many years ago was one of two things Indira truly appreciated from her father. That and his part in bringing her into the world. Emaza was two years older than her, making her twenty-six, and even though she resided in Portland, Oregon, she always made contacting Indira every two weeks a priority.

"You ask me what you're supposed to do? Well, I say kick her ass to the curb, but because you're so adamant on helping her, the least you could do is talk to her. Make her realize that she can't keep on taking your kindness for weakness. She needs to appreciate all the things that you do for her and more. All the things you do for Noah too. You're more of a mother to him than she is!"

"Em..."

"What?" Emaza gave her an unbothered look. "It's true! I know it, and you know it too." She then drank her beverage while watching the torn expression plastered on Indira's face.

One thing Emaza knew for definite was how much this situation with her mother affected Indira, but she liked to pretend that it didn't bother her that much. It was a coping mechanism that Emaza wished she would drop, especially because it wasn't helping the situation. What was the point of pretending like something truly wasn't affecting you?

"Just man up and talk to her, Indi. That's your mother, and you need to be vocal about the issues you have with her."

Indira simply nodded before taking another sip of her drink.

"Enough about your mother. How's Javon's dad doing?"

"Much better," Indira simply responded, relief suffusing her features at the change of subject of their conversation.

While they talked about Javon's father and Javon himself, Indira was unable to stop thoughts of Bakari creeping into her mind. It didn't help that her excitement levels to see him this weekend, once Emaza was on a flight, were growing each day. She wanted to see that man more than seeing Javon come home from spending the week at his father's.

It was definitely the sex that had her hooked. Indira was fully aware of that without a doubt. Although, what also had her hooked was being in his presence. Just being with him brought her a thrill and glow like no other. He enticed feelings within her that not even Javon could bring. With or without the sex, when it came to Bakari, she felt like she was on cloud nine. And that's what honestly scared her the most.

How could she feel so strongly about someone she barely knew? Yeah, they'd had a past, but a past of barely speaking to one another. Now things had changed vastly because they weren't just talking but also fucking.

A small part of Indira was truly tempted to tell her god sister about Bakari. She wanted to know if it was crazy to be feeling this way about him after hardly knowing him. But she didn't need to be a genius to know that it was crazy. What was even more craziest was what she was doing with Bakari. It was an affair, and Emaza would call her out on it immediately. She wouldn't praise her for stepping out on her fiancé but scold her because Emaza loved Javon. Everyone loved Javon. In their eyes, he treated Indira good, so what wasn't there to love?

The only thing was, no one knew about Javon's slip ups. It wasn't something Indira had told to anyone, not even Emaza. Firstly, it was embarrassing for her to have to experience her man wanting someone other than her. So that was why she never came clean to anyone. That was why he was the perfect man in Emaza's mind because she believed he had never cheated.

The journey home proved to be a bigger challenge for Indira because, of course, never-ending thoughts of Bakari consumed her mind. However, when she stepped through the door of her home, she managed to make them all disappear when she laid eyes on Javon.

"It's a Tuesday," she announced as she shut the door behind her. "What are you doing here?"

"Well, hello to you too, Indira," Javon sternly replied as he got up from the couch.

Indira gave him a blank expression and waited for him to speak up. It was a Tuesday which meant that he was supposed to be at his Dad's. She hadn't even seen the coupe parked outside for her to already realize he was here.

"My brother took over for today, so I came to spend the night with you," Javon explained with as scowl on his face. "But I see that that's now impossible when we have guests over that you never told me about."

Just as Javon finished talking, Siobhan walked into the living room with Noah in her arms.

"Oh yeah," Indira said nonchalantly. "I forgot."

"You forgot to tell me that you would be letting your mother move into our house?" Javon's scowl only got stronger.

"It's temporary," Siobhan spoke up as she set Noah down on the ground. Instantaneously, he ran up to Indira, who happily picked him up into her arms.

"Indira, we have a one-bedroom apartment," Javon said, ignoring Siobhan's words. "There's barely enough space for you and me, and now you're letting your mother move in?"

And who's fault is that? You're the reason we're still in this tiny ass apartment, Indira mused with anger.

"It's not a problem at all," Indira replied with a smile plastered on her lips as Noah gazed into her eyes.

"How is that not a problem? Where the hell are we going to sleep, Indira?" Javon questioned her with his jaw tightening.

"In our bedroom," Indira voiced simply as she began walking to the kitchen. "My mother has no problems sleeping on the couch when you're here."

"When I'm here?" Javon's fury was laced in his deep voice. "You mean to tell me you're sleeping on the couch when I'm not here?"

With Noah still in her arms, Indira walked into the kitchen and headed to the white fridge. The cold air instantly hit them both as she opened its door.

"Yup."

"Indira, this ain't right. She shouldn't be he—"

Bam!

Indira slammed the fridge door shut and decided to end this conversation already.

"Are you paying the rent of this house, Javon?"

Her question made him stare at her with a dumbfounded look, and his face went blank.

"No, bu—"

"Exactly what I thought," she fumed, giving him a poker face. "So you have no say on who gets to stay here, because you aren't paying rent in this house, Javon. Worry about your father, and I'll worry about my mother. Thanks."

Once she had said her last sentence, she walked off with Noah still holding her tight, leaving Javon with rage bottled up inside him.

Chapter Eleven

"Finally, you let me finish this piece," Arjana commented as she dipped her tattoo needle into her ink tray. Happiness coursed through her as she prepared herself to finish the tattoo piece on her current client.

"Been busy, Janny. You know this."

A client that was very close and special to her heart. To hear him call her by the nickname he had given her years ago and refused to stopped calling her, despite her complaints, warmed her heart greatly.

"Yeah, I know, Kari. It's good to be able to finish this now though," she told her brother before lowering herself down closer to his back.

The only ink that Bakari had on his skin was a large tribal pattern on the left side of his back done by Yasir years ago. On his right side was a lion piece that Arjana had outlined a few months back. Today, she was having the chance to finish shading her lion piece on her brother, and her excitement was through the roof. It was a tattoo that she wanted to get finished for ages now because she couldn't wait to see the end result of her work.

"How are you?" Bakari queried curiously as she began tatting his skin with ink. The pain was minimal for him, because she was only shading in the remainder of his tattoo. "I feel like we haven't chopped it up in a minute."

Arjana hummed in agreement before speaking up. "Yeah, it's been a minute. I'm okay though. Just grinding hard... living my life..."

"With Yasir," Bakari muttered quietly, but Arjana heard him and lightly slapped the back of his head. "Yo, chill," he warned her with a chuckle. "What's good between you two though? You back together now?"

Bakari was no stranger to Yasir and Arjana's relationship. He was fully aware of their complicated yet tight bond. When Yasir first spiked an interest in Arjana, the first person he knew that he had to go to was Bakari. There was no way that Yasir could pursue Arjana without having a conversation with Bakari. He ended up surprised but elated to know that Bakari had given him the blessing he needed.

"No," Arjana mumbled while carefully shading in the lion's face. "I don't want to get back with him."

"You sure about that?"

"...Ye... No," she responded. "Honestly, I don't know. One minute I hate him, and the next, he's all I wa... Man, I can't be talking to you about my situation with your boy."

"Says the fuck who?" Bakari queried with dismay. "You're my sister, Arjana, and you always come first. As your brother, I'm here to listen to you whenever and wherever you want. Don't feel like you ever need to keep shit from me. Matter fact, you shouldn't keep shit from me, period."

Bakari was quiet, but once he actually engaged in a deep conversation with someone, he always had meaningful things to say. More than ever, Arjana really appreciated his brotherly, protective nature. So she poured her entire heart out to him. Telling him her current doubts and conflicting feelings about Yasir.

Arjana just didn't know if they were healthy for each other. When they were together, they argued all the time about insignificant stuff. Insignificant stuff like Arjana's insecurities about Yasir's "fans" who only wanted a tattoo done by him because they found him attractive. Insignificant stuff like Yasir's baby mother always seeming to call when Arjana was trying to spend quality time with her man. However, now looking back at it all, they were all pointless arguments. Arjana also wanted to stay focused on saving for her new tattoo spot, because her dream was to open her own spot.

At the end of the day, all Bakari wanted was for his younger sister to be happy. He knew that her and Yasir had their flaws, but they made each other happy, plus, they were a great couple.

"Just do what you know and feel in your heart is right," Bakari advised. "This is your life, and only you truly know what you want. Don't force yourself to be in a relationship with him, but at the same time, don't force yourself to not be in a relationship. Take a real long time to truly think about what's best for you; weigh up the pros and cons to help you decide. In my opinion, if the pros outweigh the cons, then that's your answer right there. And if they don't? Then, shit, you know your answer still."

Arjana carefully contemplated his advice and couldn't help but smile to herself.

"You know you give me the best advice, Kari?"

"I know," he boasted cockily with a happy sigh. "You should be paying me for my services right now."

"Oh really?"

"Yup. But 'cause you're my sis, I guess a nigga gotta give you the free family service."

Arjana giggled lightly and continued to shade the rest of his tattoo in. In just under two hours, she was done, and the pair of them were admiring her work in the mirror.

"Damn, Janny," Bakari remarked with amazement. "You did a great ass job."

And that was the honest truth. The lion tattoo that now sat on his muscular back looked extremely realistic and 3D. It was as if it was about to jump off his flesh.

"I'm glad you like it," Arjana stated. "Let me take a few pictures, and I'll get you bandaged up."

Just as Arjana left Bakari by the mirror, two quick knocks sounded on her booth door, and in stepped the man that they were talking about earlier.

"Speak of the devil himself," Bakari announced, smirking at his sister as he turned to face her.

"Who?" Yasir asked, confusion fixed on his face.

"No one." Arjana glared nastily at her brother.

Yasir glanced at Arjana suspiciously before deciding to drop the subject all together.

"Yo, B. I gotta holla at you about something."

Yasir's announcement made Bakari's smirk fade, and his face switched into seriousness. Just from the tone in Yasir's voice, he knew it was something important. He gave him a simple head nod before looking at his sister who was already heading to the door.

"I'll give you two some privacy then," she voiced while walking to the doorway of where Yasir stood.

He had a sexual gaze as he looked her up and down. Just before she could slip away past him, he reached for her hand and gently kissed it, making her smile. Once she had left the room, Yasir started talking.

"He's back in town," Yasir announced reluctantly, knowing that this conversation was only going to send Bakari into a foul mood.

A foul mood was an understatement, because his face twisted into pure rage.

"Where the fuck was he?"

"Near downtown," Yasir stated. "Apparently, he's here on a quick business trip and should leave by the end of the week."

"He better," Bakari snapped. "Because if I lay eyes on him myself, it's about to be hell."

Yasir nodded knowingly before adding, "He'll be gone by the end of the week, B. For sure. You won't lay eyes on him, because I would have first and handled him accordingly."

Bakari sighed deeply before giving Yasir one last stare then deciding to examine his back tattoo in the mirror again.

"But on a brighter note, since the shop's reopened, we can start cleaning any money we need to again."

"Sounds like a plan," Bakari said in agreement. "That will take the pressure off the construction company."

Bakari's construction company was something he had started up two years ago. It was his pride and joy and meant absolutely everything to him. He had hired a loyal team of workers who were obedient and hard workers. Knowing that he could count on them to get jobs done without him being present brought a fulfilling feeling to his heart. He had built a company that could smoothly exist with or without his presence.

"Exactly," Yasir responded. "And with how fast shit moved last time, we're gonna need to clean more."

Bakari nodded in agreement as he thought about how fast the product from his plug had moved so quickly. Business was always booming but even more than usual.

Selling drugs hadn't always been his hustle. As a matter of fact, Bakari had told himself years ago that he would never resort to that lifestyle. Seeing his mother and father struggling to look after him and Tokyo and keep the lights on, broke his heart. He got a regular weekend job while in high school to help his parents pay the bills, but that wasn't enough. A dreaded day came when they received an eviction notice and had seven days to move out. With nowhere to stay and no one to turn to, Bakari's parents checked them into a hotel for the two nights they could afford. Then they were forced to sleep in the streets of Atlanta. It was their first night being homeless that changed him. He knew from that day onward, he was going to have to resort to the one thing that he never thought he would do. Now, here he was. Today, he reigned as not just the biggest drug dealer in Atlanta, but the most influential in Georgia hands down. He was the connect, and if you wanted the finest, high quality supply of pure crack cocaine or cannabis, then he was your man.

It wasn't his dream career, but it had helped him do the number one goal in his life: take care of his entire family. Being homeless was an experience that he would ensure never happened again.

Once their conversation was done, Yasir stepped out, and Arjana came back into the room to take photographs of Bakari's tattoo before bandaging him up.

Twenty minutes later, Bakari was fully clothed and driving home in his Aston Martin. Today had been a long day indeed, and the one thing he could use was some sleep. While he drove through the streets of Atlanta to head to his home on the outskirts of the city, he had an incoming call come in from his mother.

"Bakari Marshall, where have you been?"

"Mom... Sorry, I've been busy."

"Too busy to give your mother a call?"

"Mom, it ain't even like that. I've just been working with the company and... you know."

"I know," she replied with a deep sigh. "I miss you."

"Miss you more. How's Dad?"

"Why don't you ask him right now yourself? You're on loud speaker."

"Ki sa ki nan, pitit gason? *(What's up, son?)*"

"Ki sa ki nan, papa? Ou bon? *(What's up, Dad? You good?)*

Hearing the voices of his parents truly meant the world to him. They were the two most important people in his life, and he would never stop cherishing them. Hanifah and Asani Marshall were his everything.

The drive home became easier as Bakari conversed with his parents about life and work. It was only when his mother was about to bring up the subject of his love life that Bakari had pulled up into the driveway of his home, only for him to see an unexpected guest sitting by his door.

"Mom... I'm gonna need to call you back."

"What? Why? Is everything okay?" Hanifah quickly asked her son, getting anxious at the thought of something happening to him.

"Yeah, everything's fine," Bakari reassured her gently. "I've just got to tend to someone right now."

Bakari ended the call with his mother, cut off his car engine, and left his car with a warm, fuzzy feeling in his heart.

The second he got out, she stood up and innocently locked eyes with him. Seeing him walk toward her made desire course through her veins. He was dressed casual in a white t-shirt, denim jeans, and all white J's on his feet.

There was something effortless about the way he appealed to her without even doing too much. Just by seeing him walk made her want him. When he was directly in front of her, she expected him to say something, but instead, all he did was keep a locked gaze on her.

"Aren't you go..."

Before she could finish her sentence, Bakari grabbed her waist and pulled her closer into him. Then he pressed his lips against hers to embrace her soft flesh. The kiss was urgent yet sweet at the same time, confirming to Indira that coming to see him was a good idea after all. Once he pulled away from her, Indira felt weak in the knees and giddy in her heart.

"What?" he questioned her, wanting her to finish what she was saying.

"Aren't you going to ask me why I'm here?" She stared up at him with curiosity.

"Nah," he simply replied. "We both know why you're here." He pecked her lips one last time before walking around her to get to his front door.

Indira's face scrunched up, puzzlement filling her as he walked away from her. She quickly turned around to query him. "You know why I'm here?"

By now, he had his key in the door and was about to turn it until she spoke up. He turned around to face her while his key remained in the door.

"Of course I do," he confirmed cockily. "You missed me."

The smirk now forming on his lips made Indira playfully roll her eyes at him.

"No I didn't," she lied.

"Oh really? You didn't miss me?"

"No," she quietly said, knowing deep down that she had indeed missed him.

Bakari then whipped his head back around to face the door and finally opened it with his key. Once it was opened, he stepped into his home and stood in the doorway.

"Come closer and tell me how much you didn't miss me to my face," he lightly ordered as he turned to face her again.

"Gladly," she smugly stated, sauntering over to his front door. He had started a challenge that she clearly wanted to finish. The only thing was, she had no idea that this challenge was one she wouldn't succeed at.

Indira finally got in front of him, about to speak up, when she felt her body suddenly being pulled in. And before she knew it, she was in his home, the door was shut behind her, and she was pushed against his golden oak door. She felt him lift both of her thighs up onto his torso, and then he pressed himself between her center, sending her mind into a complete frenzy.

"Shit," she whispered to herself as she felt his member directly on her pearl. The member that she had greatly missed. It hadn't even been more than two days since they had seen each other last. She gazed into his pupils only to see pure lust within them.

"You wanna tell me who you didn't miss?" he firmly asked her, pressing against her harder so that she had nowhere to run. She was forced up against his door with his erection pressed into her. "I asked you a fuckin' question, Indira."

"Bakari... ple—"

"No, answer me," he demanded. "Don't try to get all shy and weak now. Tell me exactly who you didn't miss, Indira."

She hated how possessive and dominant he was because it made her succumb to him every single time.

"I missed you, Mr. Marshall," she admitted softly.

"Oh, you did, huh?" His hands slid up her thighs until they reached the back of her half-risen skirt. "Is that why you came to see me in this sexy, short ass skirt of yours?"

He had noticed it from the second he laid eyes on her. How could he not? It fit her perfect body well and revealed her long thick legs.

"Yes," she whispered, sighing softly when she felt him lift up her skirt. Her head was now clouded with hunger for him, and she knew that the only remedy was to satisfy her appetite for him swiftly. "I couldn't stop thinking about you... about him," she admitted as she looked down to stare at his bulge. "I missed you being inside me, Bakari."

One thing that he had noticed about Indira was how she always knew the right things to say to him. His plan had been to punish her for lying about not missing him in the beginning. However, now he couldn't bring himself to do it. Not yet anyways. She had charmed him with that sweet, irresistible voice of hers, and seconds later, he was on his knees eating her like his life depended on it.

"Ahhh... Ba... Bakari! ... Ssshit... Bakar... Bakari... ugh, fuck! P-Please... uhh!"

"You know... exactly what... you need to do, Di," he informed her between the pushes of his tongue inside her tight slit.

"Plea... ahh, I can't... I can't take it."

Bakari released his tongue out of her pussy so he could stare up at her from where he was on his knees.

"You can, and you will," he bossed up. "You know I ain't stopping 'til you cum on my mothafuckin' face. You a weak ass bitch now?"

Indira shook her head no in response to his question.

"That's what I fuckin' thought. So shut the hell up and ride my face," he concluded before diving his tongue back between her folds and devouring her addictive nectar. "Matter fact, turn the fuck around so I can eat my pussy from the back. Now."

Indira quickly did as he ordered, turning around and gasping when she felt him press her hard against his door. His tongue thrusted back inside her, and she almost lost it once she felt him push a finger into her butt.

"Bakari!"

"Why you... acting like you can't... take this shit, huh?" he questioned her between his tongue fucks and rapid finger pushes.

"I-I can't!" she whimpered loudly.

"You can, and you will," he affirmed. "We ain't done here until you make that pussy cum for me. And even then, we still ain't done 'cause I'm taking you upstairs, tying you up, and giving you this dick 'til you can't walk straight, Indira. That's your punishment for saying you didn't miss me."

Indira couldn't articulate the right words to say back to him, because all she found herself doing was moaning louder and louder. The pleasure only got stronger, and she knew any minute, her release would come bursting through. This man had her wrapped around his fingers, and as much as she hated it, she adored it.

Chapter Twelve

Honestly, I'm tryna stay focused

You must think I've got to be joking when I say

I don't think I can wait
I just need it now
Better swing my way

It was 11 a.m., but that didn't stop Tokyo from running errands on a Thursday morning. One thing about Tokyo's Slay Spot was that her workers were loyal and trustworthy. She could depend on them to open up the salon and run it without her being present. The salon was a smooth sailing operation, and that was one of the main reasons why it was so successful today.

Girls can't never say they want it
Girls can't never say how
Girls can't never say they need it
Girls can't never say now

Tokyo kept her attention ahead as her music blasted in her ears.

She was currently in line at Starbucks awaiting to get to the front counter to order her Iced Caramel Latte. Running errands since 9 a.m. had been tiring, and all she really wanted at this point was a drink to wake her up.

Tokyo stood patiently in the waiting area for her latte, too preoccupied with her music currently in her ears to notice the figure that had crept up a short distance behind her.

When she got called to collect her drink, Tokyo stepped forward and happily took it before turning around to lay eyes on his attractive face.

Oh my...

He had a grin on his face as he examined her and allowed his eyes to linger down her body. Seeing her in the tightest pink sundress was making his third leg between his thighs grow rapidly. It fit the curve of her hips perfectly and complemented her petite frame well. Not to mention, the color pink was everything on her.

"Well if it isn't the woman with the special touch."

Just as his lips started moving, Tokyo pulled out her left AirPod to properly hear him. His words made her crack a small smile, remembering their flirty moment at the salon.

"Hey," she friendly greeted him, unsure of what to really say in response to his words.

"Craving Starbucks, I see," he stated as he looked down at the beverage in her hands.

"Yeah," she responded, lifting up her latte. "It's the addiction I can't get enough of."

"What did you get?"

"A caramel latte," she told him simply.

"How it taste?"

"It tastes amazing," she explained wholeheartedly. "That's why I'm constantly back here getting it. It tastes good."

A sudden smirk grew on his lips, and it made Tokyo wonder what he was finding amusing. She was about to ask when she felt her phone vibrate in her palm, and she looked down to see a message from Arjana, asking her if she was free later on.

"It was nice bumping into you again," she said as she broke eye contact with him to look down at her phone. She began to type her text.

"Likewise," he said coolly, stepping closer to her.

Tokyo stopped typing to stare back up at him only to see how close he was. His seductive aroma filled her nostrils.

"I'll tell you what though," he whispered into her ear that was without an AirPod. "I bet that latte don't taste half as good as you do."

Without even being able to stop herself, Tokyo felt her insides heat up, and her mind clouded with desire. She was speechless as she looked up into his eyes to see the want he had for her. When she opened her lips in an attempt to say something, anything at all, her phone vibrated once again in her palm.

"You better tend to that," he voiced with that sexy smirk of his still plastered on his lips.

"Adonis!" the Starbucks worker called out loud, and he stepped around Tokyo to head to the collection counter.

It made her realize that she had only found out his name now. She hadn't known it before because he hadn't mentioned it. And now that she thought deeper about it, she had never asked. But now that she knew it, she never wanted to stop hearing it. He had such a beautiful name.

Ding!

Drinks tonight, pleaseeee. I need to get drunk, Yasir's driving me crazy.
Arjana.

Tokyo slowly typed back: *Sounds like a plan sis.*

She was tempted to turn around and wait for Adonis, but another part of her was reminding herself on her promise. Her promise to stay focused on being celibate. So she decided to walk toward the exit and head out of Starbucks.

Why is it that you're sending a fine ass man into my life when you know I'm trying to just do me? Why, Lord? Tokyo talked to God as she walked into the open parking lot and headed to her BMW i8. She knew that God was testing her, and the only thing she could do was prove to him that she was about to pass this test with flying colors.

"So you were about to leave without saying goodbye?"

Hearing his deep voice from behind her made her entire body

freeze. She could no longer reach into her Gucci side bag for her car keys.

Tokyo slowly turned around to see him. He had a locked gaze on her, but that didn't stop her from admiring him.

Fuck he looks good.

Adonis was wearing a tight fitted khaki t-shirt that covered his upper body like a second skin. He had a muscular physique that she was undeniably attracted to. There was just something about seeing a man with perfectly sized muscular arms that made Tokyo weak all over.

"I had to tend to my business," she informed him boldly, reminding him of his prior words before she had walked away from him.

"Yeah, but now I want you to tend to me," he replied with a firm look.

"Is that right?" Tokyo queried amusingly. "You hardly know me."

"I know enough, Tokyo," he mentioned her name, surprising her. "Enough to know that I want you."

"How do you know my name?"

"Says the woman with the biggest salon in Atlanta named after herself."

Tokyo just continued to stare at him with amazement before speaking up. "You still don't know me well enough to know that you want me, Adonis. I could be a psychopath."

"Well, shit, let's be psychopaths together, princess. You can be a psycho as much as you want around me. Be a psycho all on this..." His words trailed off quietly, and Tokyo was curious to hear him continue.

"Psycho all on what?"

"I don't want to offend you," Adonis admitted.

"You won't. Just man up and finish your sentence."

Hearing her taunt him to man up made Adonis lose his shy streak.

"Be a psycho all you want on this dick," he bluntly announced.

His announcement made her heart flutter, but she chose to give him a blank stare, trying to convince him that she was unbothered by his words. As a matter of fact, she had a little announcement of her own.

"This pussy will fuck your world up, little boy."

"Fuck it up then, princess," he fired back with the same blank stare she delivered.

His response made her break into a helpless smile and release a light laugh.

"And I plan to show you just how much of a little boy I ain't," he commented, still gazing at her.

"And when does this plan of yours commence?"

"Right now if you want it," he said as he began walking up to her. Seeing him move closer to her made her step back until she felt her car door pressed against her lower back.

"Adonis, n..."

Seeing the mixture of lust and fright in her eyes made him release a light chuckle as he came to a halt in front of her.

"I'm playing," he whispered with a smile in his eyes.

Tokyo took a deep breath as he towered over her.

"What you doing tonight?" he asked her curiously.

"Heading out for drinks with my sister."

"Wrong answer," he told her with a light head shake. "You're heading out but not with your sister."

"With who?"

"With me," he voiced. "I'll come get you around nine."

"Come get me where? You don't even know where I live."

"You're going to tell me exactly where you live so I can pick you up for our date tonight, princess."

"What if I don't want to go on this date?"

"Then tell me to get the fuck out of your face, and I swear I'll do just that."

Their tense gaze lingered on, and deep down, Tokyo knew that she would be doing anything but telling him to leave her alone. This man right here had erupted a fire inside her that she had missed. A fire that she didn't want to put out anytime soon, so quite frankly, she was going to let it burn.

"So you're ditching me for some new dick? Wow, I see how it is."

"Anaaaaa," Tokyo whined as she observed her sister through her bright screen. She was currently on FaceTime with Arjana explaining why she wasn't going to get drinks with her tonight. "It ain't even like that."

"Oh, so what's it like then?" Ana asked her with a disappointed look. "You were supposed to get drunk with me tonight; instead, you're going out to hop on some new dick. What happened to you being celibate?"

"Nothing," Tokyo voiced. "I'm still celibate."

"Ha!" Arjana instantly scoffed. "What did you say his name was? Adonis? Yeah, if he looks as sexy as his name sounds, then we both know you're no longer going to be celibate tonight."

"I hardly know the guy, Ana. There's no way in hell I'm having sex with him. On our first date? Come on, now. We're just going to get to know each other better and enjoy each other's company. I don't care how fine he is; he's not getting between these thighs."

Everything that Tokyo had told her sister was something that she was completely convinced on. But little did she realize that her convincing words were soon going to mean nothing.

She was picked up in a Maybach limo around nine by a chauffeur who introduced himself as Preston. Preston then told her that he was here under the instruction of Adonis Dawson to collect her and take her to the location of their date.

Of course, Tokyo wasn't one to just hop into a car with someone who she didn't know. But the second she was about to question Preston more about his duties for the night, a text came through from the one man who was running across her mind.

Get in the car, princess. I promise he won't kill you.
Adonis.

The first thought that came into her head was how on earth did he know that she was apprehensive about getting into the limo? Nonetheless, his text had her convinced, and she got inside without any doubts or fears.

The drive to the unknown location was half an hour. She knew this because she had been constantly watching her iPhone's clock while browsing through her phone.

"Ma'am, we're here."

Tokyo looked at Preston's cute chocolate face through the front view mirror before taking a glance out the passenger side window. From what she could see, Preston had pulled up to a restaurant.

"Thank you," she said with a small smile, reaching for the car's handle and about to open it until Preston spoke up.

"Just head inside the restaurant and someone will lead you to the roof."

"The roof?" She gave him a confused expression.

"Yeah, the roof," Preston confirmed with a smirk. "That's where your date is."

The date was in fact on the roof of the seafood restaurant, and when Tokyo was led by a friendly female waitress to the rooftop, she laid eyes on an unexpected sight.

"Oh my... Adonis... this is... this is..."

She couldn't believe it. This was only their first date, but here he was, pulling out all the stops to show her that he was serious about wanting her.

The rooftop was decorated with red roses, candles, and in the center of the rooftop was a candlelit dinner for two with a champagne ice bucket. But that wasn't even the best part. The best part was the fact that there was a band of jazz artists performing on the sidelines. Jazz that sounded so soothing and alluring to the ears.

"This is what?" he asked her as he walked over from the rooftop edge toward her.

Even seeing him again was making her heart race with anticipation. He was dressed in a black silk shirt with matching black pants. There was just something about seeing him in all black that turned her on in the worst way right now. She could see from under his left sleeve, his arm of tattoos was peeking out. He had on silver diamond studs in each ear with a matching silver cross chain sitting around his neck. Seeing his mouth open when he spoke revealed the iced-out silver grill on his bottom teeth. To put it simply, he looked mouthwatering, and Tokyo was becoming tempted at the thought of drinking him all up, although she quickly shook it off when she remembered her promise to herself.

"This is amazing," she complimented him, finishing off her words.

By now, he had strolled over to her and was standing right in front of her.

"You look amazing," he complimented her back, biting his lips as he stared her up and down.

She blushed at his compliment before thanking him. Then he reached for her hand, gently led her to her seat, pulling out her chair and waiting for her to sit before he went to his own seat.

The more Tokyo stayed in his presence, the more she found herself more attracted to him. He knew how to hold a conversation effortlessly well and get her to open up to him. With just a few words, he had Tokyo almost telling him her entire life story.

Yeah, I want him, she mused as she placed her champagne flute to her lips. It wasn't a thought she had been able to stop herself from thinking. The more she stayed in his presence, the worse it got for her. *Snap out of it, T. You're staying celibate for an entire year. Don't fuck this up.*

"I hope you liked the food," Adonis announced in an intrigued tone. "I had the chief prepare it 'specially for us."

"I loved it," she revealed as she beamed at him. "The shrimp was delicious."

Adonis kept a fixed gaze on her while finessing his fingers through his beard. Watching him gently stroke his hair made Tokyo wish that those fingers were stroking somewhere else.

"You got enough space for desert?" Adonis queried while raising a brow at her.

"I sure do," Tokyo said. "Do you?"

"Oh 100 percent," he replied. "I'm more than ready for my desert."

Just by the sexual tone that she could hear him speaking in made

Tokyo's center pulsate excitedly. She had to keep her thighs tightly pressed against each other in the hopes that she would calm down.

"What's for desert?" she wondered aloud, half of her wanting to know, but the other half just wanting to keep the conversation moving along so that she could ease the tension she could feel between them.

"I'm hoping you are," Adonis boldly stated, his pearly whites and diamond grill flashing at her as he spoke. "'Cause you're all I want to taste for the rest of tonight."

Shit.

Tokyo stared at him with shock but also lust. Intense lust that she could no longer conceal. All throughout their conversation, she had felt the lust slowly building, but now it had reached a peak that could not be broken.

Everything that Tokyo had told her sister hours ago on the phone went out the window in twenty minutes. Because twenty minutes later, Tokyo was back in the Maybach limo that had come to pick her up courtesy of him. Only this time, Adonis sat right next to her.

He was looking at her like he wanted to eat her up, and it lowkey scared her. Usually she was the one that called all the shots in the bedroom and told men exactly how, where, and when she wanted them to taste her. Now she couldn't dare to utter a word while he gazed at her. This man was dangerous because he had her under his spell without saying anything right now.

When his hand landed on her exposed thigh and traveled up her leg, Tokyo felt her entire body warm up by his single touch.

"Adonis, I..."

Her words were incomplete when his lips came in her direction, and he pressed his soft flesh to hers. It was surprising yet happily welcomed by her, because all night, Tokyo had wanted to feel his thick lips against hers. While their lips moved in loving harmony, his hand moved higher up her thigh until he reached her middle.

Tokyo internally moaned when she felt his hand press into her soft core, feeling into the wetness of her thong. He gently pulled their lips apart only to stare into her eyes.

"You're soaking, princess," he voiced in a pleased tone.

Tokyo shyly stared back at him, sighing softly at his fingers now massaged her folds through the lace of her thong.

"Adonis..."

"What?" he whispered before pressing his lips on her neck then down to her collarbone.

The off the shoulder, body hugging red dress she had opted for tonight meant that Adonis hadn't been able to take his eyes off her. He hadn't been able to stop thinking about clearing that table and dicking her down immediately. Fuck the jazz band he had hired and the waiter. But remembering that he couldn't be so obscene yet on their first date made him shake the idea away.

"I'm not sure this is a good idea... This is our first date, and we're just getting to know each other. I haven't had sex in a while because I promised myself I was going to remain celibate and just focus on myself for a while. I've been known to go crazy over guys, and I just wanted to chill on all of that and just be free from guys. I'm supposed to be doing me."

Her announcement made him look up her neck and glance at her carefully. Those mahogany pools staring hard at her made Tokyo feel coy once again under his gaze.

Instead of him saying anything in response to her, Adonis carefully reached for her right hand and pulled it over to his lap. Tokyo looked down with interest to see what he was trying to do. When he pushed her hand down to the center of his pants, she helplessly gasped when she felt his growing member.

"You feel that shit?" Adonis's deep voice was sounding like a sweet lullaby in her ears. "You feel what you've done to me?" Tokyo's heart skipped a beat, but to her it felt like it had skipped several. "You feel how hard I am because of you? How hard this dick has gotten from watching you all night and not being able to touch you?" All Tokyo found herself doing was staring down at his bulge and feeling it grow more under her palm.

"I plan to be in your guts tonight, Tokyo. I plan to make you scream my mothafuckin' name until it's the only thing you know. And I plan to be the last nigga that gets to blow your back out every night.

Believe that, princess. 'Cause ain't no nigga after me. I'm your last nigga and forever nigga."

The sweetest lullaby was all Tokyo could hear being uttered from his lips. Nothing else. And it was his words that confirmed to her that being celibate was no longer on the table.

"Aghhhhhh, Adonis!"

So she followed him back to his house and let him clap her shit like a standing ovation.

"Take this dick, princess," he ordered. "Take it fuckin' all."

The faster he pounded into her, the better it felt. But with it feeling good also came the pain. It was a pain that she loved feeling though. The only thing was, the quicker he drilled into her, the more Tokyo could feel her frontal wig start to slip.

The sweat that had formed all over her body had also formed on her forehead and scalp which meant that her hair glue to lay down her frontal had melted away.

"Adon... Adon... shit!"

Feeling air hit her head made her eyes pop open, and she yelped out. Her frontal wig had flown off her head, and now more than ever, she was mortified. However, instead of Adonis stopping like she expected him to, he just continued to pump himself deeper inside her.

His eyes opened widely to stare down at her wigless head. He noticed her scrambling to get it and quickly placing it on her head, which was a struggle for her to do properly because of his never-ending strokes.

"Uhhh, Adon... Ad... Sslo... slow, oh shit!"

"Fuck no," he snapped with groans. "I ain't slowing down. Matter fact..."

Adonis snatched her wig off her head only to straighten it in his hands before wrapping it around her throat and pulling her up closer to him while he hit her pussy from the back.

Tokyo felt her juices instantly flow quicker down her thighs, and she was shocked at herself for being turned on by what he had just done. He had suddenly grabbed her wig and was now choking her with it.

"Adonis, mmhhh, fuck," she moaned loudly.

Adonis only smirked to himself as he whispered into her ear, "Ain't no slowing down. I told you before that you gon' take this dick, so that's exactly what you're gonna do. Don't make me fuck you up, Tokyo."

And before she knew it, he pushed her back down against the mattress so that her face was forced against pillows. Then he continued to powerfully fuck her until she climaxed nonstop for him.

It was at this moment that Tokyo knew she was going to become a psychopath. His psychopath.

Chapter Thirteen

M*eet me outside.*
    Back door.
Bakari.

You're here? she quickly texted back. *Why?*

Bakari: *Meet me outside, Indira. This isn't up for discussion.*

Deciding to just obey his words, Indira tidied up her work space and grabbed her bag before heading out the back door. Her lunch break had just started, leaving her free for just over an hour. Her plan hadn't been to leave work, she was going to browse Uber Eats and request something from the app. However, now Bakari had requested to meet her, so getting a takeaway would have to be a late evening thing.

Going through the back door and seeing him in his Aston Martin waiting for her made her heart flutter with anticipation. She quickly walked over to his passenger side door, opened it, and took her seat next to him.

When she turned to him and saw the large smile on his handsome face, she got the sudden urge to want to sit somewhere else that wasn't on this leather seat.

"Hi," she greeted him shyly, killing the loud silence that had formed between them.

"You good?" he asked her before reaching for her hand that was on her lap and gently pulling it toward him, which ultimately pulled her up from her seat.

"Yeah," she whispered, nerves flying in her stomach once she was pulled closer to him. "You?"

"Good now that you're here with me," he explained before planting a sweet, delicate kiss on her lips. She happily received his lips, sighing softly at how great she felt kissing him. When he eventually cut their kiss short, Indira pouted with disappointment. It made him smirk to see her not wanting their intimate moment to end.

"Don't worry," he announced. "There's plenty more of that where we're going."

"Where are we going?"

"Where do you think we're going, Indira?" he questioned her back as he started the car engine.

"I don't know; that's why I'm asking you, Bakari."

"Guess," he told her with one last glance before pulling the car out of the back parking lot of Tokyo's salon.

"...I don't know," she quietly said, deep in thought. How was she supposed to know where he was taking her when he hadn't given her any hints?

"What's the one thing you want right now?"

"You," she whispered with a sexy smile.

"The other thing you want right now, Di," he said with a chuckle. "No doubt you'll get exactly what you want later, but what's the other thing your body is telling you that you need?"

"Food?"

Bakari glanced back at her with a satisfied look before focusing on his driving.

It took less than thirty minutes for Bakari to arrive at the location that he was taking her to. At first, Indira was baffled because he seemed to have pulled up to nowhere. There was only a large park that she could see off in the distance, but other than that, the place looked deserted.

"Bakari, what are we doing here?" she asked him with confusion and slight irritation. In her mind, he would be taking her to a restaurant so they could get something to eat, but he hadn't done that.

"Close your eyes."

"What? Bakari, what's go—"

"You trust me, don't you?" he asked her with a serious look. "Just close your eyes."

Indira sighed deeply before following his instruction and closing her eyes. She listened as Bakari got out from his seat and left the car, only to open up her car door and carefully get her out. He placed a hand over her eyes then he slowly guided her through the area until they suddenly came to a stop.

"Bakari," she called out to him, no longer feeling his hand over her eyes, and no longer feeling his presence around her. When he didn't reply to the call of his name, Indira started to get worried.

"Bakari!"

"Relax, Di." He chuckled as he pressed his body behind hers. "I'm right here. Open your eyes."

Indira's eyes fluttered open, and she was greeted by an unexpected sight. Laid out in front of her was a picnic mat that had various foods on plates, pillows for them to sit on, and a bottle of Moët and Chandon champagne with two empty champagne flutes.

"Bakari, this is so cute," she happily commented as she sauntered closer to the picnic. "Awww!"

Bakari observed her move closer and followed her, waiting for her to take a seat. The happiness he could hear in her voice and see within her was only making him feel more gassed. Being romantic wasn't his forte, but he wanted to step out of his comfort zone for her, the same way she had stepped out of her comfort zone for him in the bedroom.

"Awww, Bakari, this is so cute!" She complimented him once again, turning to look at him with a wide grin.

"Cut that cute shit out," he playfully snapped with a frown.

"But it is cute! You did this all by yourself?"

He gave her solid nods as a confirmation. Indira then turned her entire body around and moved nearer to him before wrapping her arms around his neck.

"This is so sweet, Bakari. I love it. Thank you."

"You welcome," he replied, wrapping his arms around her waist and pulling her tighter to him.

Their lips instantly connected, and Indira gave him the most passionate kiss she could muster, trying to show him how appreciative she was through her lips alone. Her tongue parted through his lips and settled in his mouth to begin a steamy tongue battle. She used her wet flesh to dominate his mouth and dance with his tongue.

"Shit," he cursed when she pulled their lips apart. "Fuck the food; let me keep tasting you."

Indira lightly giggled before pulling herself out of his arms, kicking off her Vans, and taking a seat on a pillow.

Bakari's picnic had fruits, cheese, sandwiches, and numerous Haitian snacks. While he poured her a glass of champagne, she reached for a snack and started feasting away.

"So is this how you seduce all the women in your life?"

"What women?" he asked her with a blank stare as he rubbed her feet.

"Women," she simply stated before taking a sip of her champagne.

"This is how I seduce the woman who is sitting right in front of me," he explained confidently, staring at her carefully. "The only woman I want in my life."

She remained silent for a while, picking up a red grape in front of her and popping it into her mouth with a grin.

"So you admit," she said between chews. "You're seducing me."

"Undoubtedly," he admitted, making her blush. "Just because I've had you doesn't mean I'm going to stop making an effort."

She gave him a pleased look before popping another grape into her mouth.

"You know you've never stopped running through my mind since the day I first met you," he revealed, making her heart skip a beat.

"W-What?"

"The first day I saw you, all those years ago, I wanted you, Indira," he explained truthfully. "But I thought you couldn't stand me when you refused my offers of dropping you home. I thought you hated a nigga, so I decided to just never say anything to you."

"I always thought you saw me as Tokyo's little friend," she

announced, shock filling her at his revelations. "So I just didn't want to bother you by making you drop me home, like it was a chore to you or something you felt forced to do."

"Nah, never that."

"So when I got back in touch with Tokyo and started working for her, you were the last person I expected to see. I thought you moved aboard or some shit."

"What did you think when you saw me?"

His question made her give him a shy smile, but she refused to answer him.

"Nah, don't get all shy now. You forget how many positions I've had you in? How many times you've sat on my face?" he questioned her firmly. "Answer me, Di."

"Do I have to?"

The seriousness within his eyes refused to go away, so she knew she was going to have to answer him.

"I was so nervous... You wouldn't stop staring, and I found myself smitten at the sight of you. You had erupted a flame within me that I just couldn't put out. 'Til this day, I still can't put it out," she honestly said, sighing softly. "What did you think when you saw me?"

"Damn that ass is fat now," he jokingly responded. Seeing the frown now on her lips made him chuckle before adding, "But seriously... I thought I was dreaming because I thought I would never lay eyes on you again. And finally getting to lay eyes on you again made me realize that I never want to stop laying eyes on you ever again. God was showing off when he made you, Indira... You're perfect."

She felt like she was floating after hearing his words. He had said the simplest yet sweetest words that were now making her gaze at him lovingly. Like he was the man that she planned to spend the rest of her life with. Instead of saying anything, she shifted closer to him before branding her lips to his, giving him a gentle peck.

"I lo..."

Her words quickly trailed off when she realized what she was about to admit. It was way too soon and didn't make any sense for her to be saying it now.

She looked away from him, embarrassed that she was about to tell him those three words too soon. However, instead of allowing her to stay looking away from him, Bakari pulled her chin back in his direction and pecked her lips once again.

"I do too," he whispered truthfully to her, stroking her skin. "I do too, Indira."

Feelings they'd had for each other for years were finally able to showcase. They were finally able to be themselves and admit the way they felt about each other. It may have seemed strange, but to them, it felt familiar. Like they had been waiting all their lives for this.

Their lips joined together again, and the both of them hungrily kissed one another. While their tongues collided, Indira felt Bakari carry her up by her waist and settle her down onto his lap. And that was when things only got more heated between them. He started squeezing on her butt while she slowly began grinding on his bulge that she was sitting on.

"Mmh, Bakari," Indira moaned when his lips left hers and started kissing down her neck.

His hands let go of her butt to reach beside him for the jar of raspberry honey that they'd used as a dip for their cinnamon rolls. Once it was in his hands, he pulled away from her neck as he brought it in front of them both.

Indira looked down at it before looking up at him with an intrigued look.

Instead of saying anything to her, Bakari decided to let his hands do all the talking. He dropped the honey between them and used both hands to lift her top off.

"Ba... Kari," she said as she allowed him to lift her top over her head. "Right here?"

"You know it," he told her with a smirk before lifting each hand to each breast that was hugged by her bra. "It's just us here, Di. Why you acting scared, like I ain't blown your back out in public before?"

His question made her remember the first ever time they'd had sex. On the balcony of Yasir's tattoo shop. Remembering the moment brought an instant smile to her face.

"See," Bakari knowingly stated as he squeezed her soft mounds before moving his hands to her back and unhooking her bra. "You forget who you are? Mr. Marshall's little, nasty..."

"Bitch." She completed his words in a soft whisper, looking down to see her now exposed breasts.

Bakari only smiled before reaching for the jar of raspberry flavored honey, opening it and pouring some onto her right nipple.

It was exhilarating for Indira to watch and feel his tongue work its magic on her nipples. Each breast he tended to lovingly, providing her with an ultimate, intoxicating pleasure.

Never in her wildest dreams would Indira have imagined having an intimate picnic in a park, getting a foot massage, and then getting honey sucked off her nipples by a sexy ass man such as Bakari. He was so different... so freaky... and she loved it.

- 1 Week Later -

"Boss lady, is everything okay?"

"Everything is fine. Why the fuck do you guys keep asking me if something's up? Nothing's up, but something will be if you guys keep on pestering me."

All day, Tokyo had been in a foul mood. She'd tried to downplay it and act like nothing was bothering her, but all her workers could clearly see that something was up.

It had been one week since she had laid eyes on Adonis. The last time she had seen him had been the day of their date and the night they'd had sex. She hadn't heard from since. Despite the fact that she had been hitting him up with texts and even called a few times, she had not gotten a single response from Adonis. And that infuriated her more than anything because it made her feel used. Like he had wined and dined her just to have sex with her. So the anger she felt because of Adonis, she took out on her workers who tried to make their usual conversation with her. She knew it was wrong, but she honestly couldn't help it. She couldn't help the anger that she felt.

"Maybe he's just busy."

"For one whole week, Ana?" Tokyo questioned her sister over the phone. "Make that make sense."

"So he's not texted you back once?"

"No," Tokyo said with dismay. "And I think I've been used."

"Really?"

"Yes!" she exclaimed. "He got what he wanted from me, and now he's off. I'm so damn stupid!"

"T, I think you're overreacting a little," Arjana voiced in a gentle tone, not wanting to set her sister off anymore. But it was too late. Tokyo was livid.

"Overreacting!" she yelled. "I let that nigga fuck on the first date. When have I ever let some random ass nigga fuck m—"

Knock! Knock!

The sound of two loud knocks cut Tokyo off, and she took a deep breath before telling whoever was on the other side to come in.

"Sorry to disturb you, T, but these came through the door addressed to you," one of her hairstylists Tae announced.

Tokyo looked at what he was holding, only to see a large bouquet of red roses in his hands.

"Oh my..."

Tokyo observed with surprise as he set the bouquet on her desk before pulling out a card and handing it over to her.

"Ana, let me call you back," Tokyo informed her sister who was still on the line.

"Alrightie," Arjana concluded before ending the call.

Tokyo reached over for the note that Tae had handed her and carefully read it.

A bouquet of roses for the beautiful rose in my life.
Adonis.

Tae swiftly turned around and headed to the door. He had already seen Tokyo's foul mood being taken out on his co-workers, and he didn't want to face the same treatment.

"Thank you, Tae," Tokyo gratefully told him as he got to her door.

"You welcome, T!"

Just as Tae had walked out, Tokyo looked down at her vibrating iPhone only to see an incoming text message from... *him.*

My apologies for not hitting you up this week, princess. Work got the best of me but I'm more than willing to make it up to you tonight.

Adonis.

Tokyo simply stared down at his text message, still not in the mood to respond to him straight away.

Princess... talk to me.

Adonis.

I'm tryna see you tonight.

Adonis.

Please princess, let me see you and show you how sorry I am.

Adonis.

She eventually gave in and hit him back with a simple: *Okay, fine. Where?*

Adonis sent her over his address, and six hours later, Tokyo had arrived at his condo. What she didn't understand was the sudden wave of nerves that hit her upon knocking on his door. And it only got worse when she was face to face with him.

It didn't help that he was shirtless and wearing gray sweatpants. His perfect chest was out, and she marveled at the sight of his well-structured abdominal muscles.

"Damn, I missed that pretty face," Adonis spoke up with a smirk.

"You missed me, but you couldn't hit me up for the entire week?" she asked with a frown.

"I was busy, pri—"

"Bullshit," she interrupted him rudely. "You probably weren't too busy to go hit up some other girl."

"Oh, so that's why you think?" His smirk only grew wider.

She gave him a light shrug before answering, "Won't be the first time a nigga's played me, and it won't be the first time I need to cut someone off before he ends up dead."

"Well I'm not like any other nigga you've been with, Tokyo," he firmly said, his smirk beginning to fade from his face. "Stop talking to me like I'm one of these other niggas. You're the only girl I'm fucking with right now and will fuck the shit out of after this conversation. I told you I was busy, and my bad for not responding to your messages, but you're here now, ain't you? So lose the attitude before I make you lose the attitude, and get your sexy ass in here so I can give you this dick."

Tokyo's knees turned to water after his words, and her eyes sparkled with hunger for him. She obediently nodded and observed as he stood out of the way for her to walk inside. When she moved into his condo and examined his modern theme living space, she felt a hard spank land on her butt.

"Get in that bedroom and take everything off but your heels. A'ight?"

"Yes, daddy."

Chapter Fourteen

K eep *Friday night free, Di.*
       We've got plans.
Pack a bag.
And wear that sexy white dress I like.
Bakari.
Indira: *A bag?*
Bakari: *Yeah a bag.*
Bakari: *Pack a few bikinis too and sexy shit you'll feel comfortable in.*
Indira: *Where are we going, Bakari?*
Bakari: *Bring your passport too.*

Excitement started to fill Indira at the thought of them travelling together. *He's taking me on vacation? Damn... wait I should probably ask him for his bank account details.*

Indira: *What's your account details?*
Bakari: *?*
Indira: *So I can pay for my flight.*
Bakari: *Are you high?*
Bakari: *You're not paying for shit, Di. Shut up.*
Bakari: *I got you always.*

Indira suddenly felt silly for even asking in the first place. It was a habit that she had picked up from Javon. Javon rarely paid for her on their prior dates, so paying for herself was just something that she was used to.

Thinking about Javon these days didn't faze her like it used to. She used to get extremely guilty when thinking about the fact that they were still engaged. But even thinking about their engagement was a rarity since she never wore her ring. She didn't even classify herself as being his fiancée anymore. What was the point? She hardly saw him because not only was he never home Monday to Friday since he was with his father, but he didn't come much on the weekends either. Indira figured it was because her mother and Noah were still living with her, and he hated it.

Not only did Indira not care about his feelings toward her mother living with her, but she was glad that he wasn't around as much. It meant that she could spend more days and nights with Bakari without worrying about Javon questioning her. Her mother never asked questions either and just minded her business. She wasn't really around either, and Indira suspected that she was back on her party girl lifestyle because she would leave the house past midnight when Noah was asleep.

Indira had enrolled Noah into pre-school which meant that he had somewhere to learn and have fun. When he wasn't in preschool, she was either babysitting him, or if she was working or with Bakari, then he would be with his mother. The only thing was since Bakari was taking her away for the week, Indira needed to let her mother know that she wouldn't be home.

"Mom," Indira called out to Siobhan as she sat outside the bathtub that Noah sat in. He was too preoccupied playing with the water to even look at his sister who had come in. "I'm going away for the weekend with a friend. I just thought I'd let you know since I won't be around."

Siobhan turned to face her with a smile.

"Oh, okay. Thanks for telling me."

"No worries," Indira responded calmly about to turn around to take her leave from the bathroom until her mother spoke up.

"Indi..." Indira locked eyes with her again. "I just want to thank you, you know. For all you've done for me and your brother. Letting us stay here for free, taking care of him without me asking... You don't have to do all that, but you do. And I know I've not been the best example of a mother to you, Indira. But thank you for everything."

Joy began to well up inside her heart as she stared at her mother. This moment right here was everything to Indira, because for the longest time, she had been putting off confronting her mother about her behavior. Emaza had pushed her to talk to her mother, but Indira could never seem to bring herself to do it. However, now that her mother had brought up the conversation, Indira felt confident enough to talk to her mother.

"Mom... you know that I love you regardless of how you act, but you need to do better."

"I know," Siobhan calmly agreed, taking a quick glance at Noah to see him still playing around in his bath water.

"I'm serious," Indira pressed on. "Not for me, but for Noah. You need to set a better example for Noah. He's still small, and he needs your constant attention, Mom. You can't neglect him like you did to..."

Indira's words trailed off when she realized what she was about to admit. Her past with her mom was a touchy subject because it involved her late brother, Kieran. But the truth was that Siobhan had neglected her kids and neglected her husband, resulting in their divorce.

"I promise I'll do better, Indi." Her mother took over the conversation. "I promise I'll make up for my past mistakes with you and your brother. I promise."

Indira sighed softly before giving her a small smile, hoping and praying that her mother actually tried to do what she promised to do.

- A Few Days Later -

Indira let out a gentle sigh and gracefully smiled as she looked up at the handsome figure now in front of her. The figure that had his hands on her shoulders, moving across to her neck before sliding up her throat and settling to hold her cheeks. His hands gently began stroking her soft skin before he leaned down to give her a sweet peck.

"I can't believe you've brought me to Cuba," Indira announced, affection glowing within her eyes as she continued to stare up at him.

"First time for everything, right?" He gave her a happy grin.

"Indeed," she responded.

Friday had finally arrived, and Indira had been picked up by Bakari. He drove them both to the airport, and they were on a business class flight to Cuba, Havana.

Business was indeed what Bakari had come to Cuba for. He needed to meet with his plug to discuss important business. Then he was free to do whatever he liked for the entire weekend. The only person he wanted to be with was Indira, so bringing her along for this trip was a perfect idea to him.

"First time for everything." Indira repeated his words and lifted her hands to his waist. "Including someone blowing my back on this bed for the first time." Her hands moved to the waistband of his gray sweats, and she was about to pull it down until Bakari grabbed her wrists. Her head instantly popped up, confusion forming in her eyes.

"Can I take a rain check?" he asked her. "I've got to head out real quick for a meeting." Indira instantly pouted at him. "Di, don't do that shit. I promise I'll be back before you know it."

"But what am I supposed to do when you're gone?"

"Neither of us have finished unpacking, so keep yourself occupied doing that, Di."

"And once I'm done doing that?"

"Change into a sexy ass bikini and wait for me. I'm taking you on a yacht."

"A yacht?" Her eyes gleamed with excitement.

"Yup," he confirmed. "And you getting this dick 'til you in a fuckin' coma."

Indira's cheeks immediately went red after his comment.

Bakari gave her one last peck before removing his hands off her face and backing away from her. He was about to head to their hotel bathroom until Indira spoke up once again.

"Does it have to be a bikini, Kari?"

He kept a locked gaze on her before asking, "What, you don't want to wear one?"

"No, I do, but... I've got a couple sundresses I want you to fuck me in."

Her announcement made his third leg grow instantly, and he looked at her lustfully.

"I see you tryna start some shit that you know can't be finished until I get back."

"Do you really have to go through, Kari?" she asked with an innocent stare as her hands traveled to the straps of the tank top she wore. "I don't want you to leave me, Bakari." She pulled her straps over her shoulders and slowly pushed her top down.

"Di, shit... I gotta go. Stop," he ordered in a low tone, unable to stop his eyes from widening at her chest. Her chest that was now exposed to him. "Please..."

Seeing the weakness in his eyes and hearing it in his voice as he stared at her breasts, made her smile with pure satisfaction.

"I promise when I get back, you're gonna get exactly what you need and more," he told her.

"And more?" She slipped him a curious eye as she raised her hands to cup both her mounds.

"Yes," he said, barely above a whisper, his body aching with the need to touch her as he observed her now stroking her breasts. "I promise, baby."

Hearing him call her baby for the first time ever, warmed her heart greatly. And was enough to make her no longer tease him and let him get ready to leave for his meeting.

When he was gone, Indira took his advice and decided to unpack both her and his belongings. One thing that she had learned about Bakari was that he loved reading books in his free time. So seeing a copy of *Things Fall Apart* by Chinua Achebe in his suitcase wasn't a surprise. What was a surprise to her was something else.

"What are..." Her words trailed off when she lifted the object out of his suitcase and into the air.

They were a pair of handcuffs which didn't surprise her because Bakari restricting her hand movement in the bedroom was nothing new. What she was surprised about was the fact that he had brought it along on their trip. Staring at them further made her develop an idea, so she decided to take the handcuffs and hold onto them.

Just over an hour later, Bakari was back from his meeting, and

Indira was dressed in a hot pink bikini with a white beach robe on top and pink side bag.

"You do know how amazing you look right now, right?"

Bakari's query made her blush, and she pecked his lips before holding onto him tighter.

After Bakari had arrived back at their hotel, it was only ten minutes later that he received a call telling him that their car was ready for them.

They had a designated Cuban driver who was to take them wherever they needed to go. Now here they were, enjoying drinks and snacks on a yacht together.

Indira sat on Bakari's lap with one hand over his shoulder while his hand was positioned in the center of her thighs.

"So how was your meeting?"

Bakari's champagne glass was on his lips, but upon hearing her question, he quickly took one last sip before lifting it away.

"Good," he responded coolly, massaging her inner thigh softly.

His meeting had gone well. Thiago Calvo was the man that supplied Bakari with the purest Cuban cocaine and cannabis. Their meeting had entailed Thiago congratulating Bakari on how well the business was moving and to also discuss Bakari's retirement plan. He had made more than enough money with Thiago, and it was getting to that point of him getting tired of selling drugs. He wanted to stay focused on his construction company and live his life without having to worry about rivals or the Feds. He also didn't want to bring children into the world when he was still moving weight. He was turning thirty in a few months, and his number one goal when he did turn thirty would be to leave the game for good.

"Just handled business, same old shit," he simply explained to her before changing the subject. "How was unpacking?"

"Interesting," Indira replied with a grin before lifting her champagne flute to her lips.

Bakari's brow shot up in the air as he watched her closely. "Interesting?"

She swallowed her rose before saying, "Yeah. Interesting."

She attempted to take more swallows until her glass was pulled down and out of her hands.

"Why was it interesting, Indira?"

The grin that had formed on her lips only grew wider, and she silently stared at him before deciding to talk again.

"I can show you better than I can tell you," she voiced seductively.

"Oh really?"

Indira moved her leg off his and slowly got up from his lap. She then started walking away from him in the deck area, toward the main cabin.

"Yeah," she said as she slowly started pulling her sheer white robe from her body, letting it drop down and exposing her bikini from behind.

She turned her head to the side momentarily, only to ask him, "You coming?"

"Without a doubt," he replied sexually as his teeth sunk into his lips.

Seeing her round, perfectly sized butt being eaten up by her bikini thong only made him harden in his pants. He quickly got up from his seat and followed her inside the yacht to the bedroom that was onboard.

Indira was surprised but delighted to learn that Bakari's yacht had a private bedroom. It only made her more eager to carry out her personal surprise for him.

When she entered the bedroom, Bakari was fast on his heels right behind her and ready to pounce on her. Until she requested for him to take a seat and shut his eyes.

"What? Why, Di?"

"It's a surprise, Kari," she simply informed him. "Please? For me?"

At first, Bakari was apprehensive, but then he decided to give in and do what she wanted. He sat by the edge of the queen-sized bed and closed his eyes for her. It was only seconds later when Bakari felt her pull his arms behind his back, and before he could react, his wrists were cuffed in place.

"Indira, what th... oh shit."

His eyes popped open and he was greeted to an amused look on her pretty face. And he knew exactly why she was amused.

"You told me to unpack your stuff," she reminded him innocently. "And I found those bad boys."

"Take them off, Di," he demanded, but Indira simply shook her head. "Now."

"No," she affirmed. "It's my turn."

"Who says you get a turn?"

"I do," she confidently said. "What's wrong with me cuffing you?"

"Take them off, Di. I'm supposed to be the one in control."

"Well I'm the one in control now," she bossed up. "So sit back and enjoy the ride, baby."

Bakari's attractive face was fixed on hers in with a serious glare. Indira knew he was going to find her idea... surprising, because he was the one in control all the time. But today, she wanted things to be different.

His face started to soften the more he observed her standing in front of him in that alluring bikini of hers. More than ever, his body ached to touch her, but he knew that today, things were going down her way.

"Draw the curtains," Bakari suddenly requested.

"The curtains?"

"Yeah." He chuckled lightly at his realization. "You don't realize what you've put on me, do you?" Indira gave him a baffled look. "Draw the curtains and you'll see."

She decided to follow his instruction and pulled the silk curtains so that no light could enter the room.

"Okay, so what is it I'll se..."

Indira's eyes grew large at the sight ahead. The handcuffs that she had placed on Bakari were now glowing brightly.

"Glow in the dark handcuffs," she whispered excitedly as she moved back to him and stared closely at his wrists.

"Yup. That's what I was planning to put on you tonight, but I see you've beat me to the punch," Bakari explained.

Indira beamed at him before reaching behind her back to untie her bikini.

"What are you going to do to me?" Bakari queried.

Indira only remained smiling, throwing her bikini to the side before sliding down her thong and stepping out of it.

"What am I going to do to you?" she repeated his question with a smirk.

"Indir—"

She cut him off instantly. "Miss Porter," she corrected him sternly.

"Miss Porter," he obediently repeated after her. "Tell me."

She gave him a lustful look, marveling at the sight of his shirtless chest and loving the look of his muscles, then she announced, "I'm going to turn you into my little, nasty bitch, Bakari Marshall, and I'm going to love every single minute of it. So shut the fuck up before I make you shut the fuck up."

Chapter Fifteen

C uba had been a weekend like no other for Indira. Other than the mind-blowing sex that her and Bakari had, the activities they had done were extremely enjoyable.

He taken her to Varadero Beach, the zoo, the aquarium, a few museums, snorkeling, and organized a private tour for them to the breathtaking capital city, Havana. The weekend had been spectacular, but for it now to be over greatly broke Indira's heart. She didn't want to switch on her phone's data and face reality.

When they had landed in Cuba, Indira decided to keep her phone on airplane mode so that any calls or texts coming in, she would not see. She especially didn't want to see Javon bombarding her with calls, asking her where the hell she was.

This trip with Bakari had only made Indira realize how deeply she was falling for this man. Falling asleep in his arms and waking up to see his face made great satisfaction course through her veins. She had also opened up to him deeply on this trip. They talked more about her family life, and the topic of Kieran came up. She talked to him about memories of her late brother and cried in his arms when he consoled her. The last thing she wanted to do was leave Bakari and head back to... Javon.

"You okay, Di?"

Indira's head snapped in his direction, and she gave him a small smile followed by a head nod.

"Nah, you gotta speak up for me, baby. What's up?" He reached for her hand and held onto her tightly.

They were currently in a car being drove by Bakari's driver away from the airport to Indira's home.

"I'm fine... It's just upsetting to know that our trip is over. I enjoyed this trip so much. Thank you."

"It doesn't have to end here," Bakari told her boldly. "Just say the word. I'll ask him to turn the car around, and we'll be back in Cuba."

"That's crazy, Kari," she said, secretly considering to tell him that so they could head back. But with all the responsibilities she had here in Atlanta, she knew that it was impossible.

It didn't matter what she had been doing with Bakari. She was still engaged to another man. Another man that Bakari no longer wanted her with.

Heading to Cuba with her had only made him more certain about his feelings for her. They were stronger and not going anywhere. There was only one thing that Bakari wanted going, and that was the other nigga in her life.

"I gotta be honest with you, Di," he spoke up boldly, "I don't want you with him anymore."

Indira felt an uncomfortable feeling creep inside her, and instead of saying anything to him, she slowly started to remove her hand out of his.

"Indira," he firmly called her, keeping her hand in his. "I don't want you with him anymore."

Silence still remained within her, and it was beginning to infuriate him.

"Did you hear what the fuck I just said?"

"Yes."

"So what aren't you answering me? I'm not fuckin' jokin' around with you, Indira."

She quickly snatched her hand out of his.

"What exactly do you want me to say, Bakari?" she asked him defensively. "I'm engaged."

"I been told you that I don't give a fuck about that engagement bullshit," he retorted. "You don't need to be with him anymore."

"Bakari, I can't just leave him."

"Why the hell not?" he questioned rudely. "You don't want to be with him anymore."

Indira sighed deeply and turned her head away from him. Their broken eye contact was brief because her chin was pulled so that her eyes were back on his.

"You don't want to be with him anymore, Di. Or do you?"

She sighed deeply again before stating, "I don't."

"So leave him," Bakari demanded.

"It's not simple, Bakari. Him and I have history together; we've been through a lot together."

"Fuck your history," he snapped. "What does history have to do with the fact that you no longer want him? What does it have to do with the fact that you want me?" Indira became silent once again, infuriating him further. "Unless you don't want me, and I've just been fooling myse—"

"No, I do want you, Bakari," she interrupted him. "You know I do. You know how I feel about you."

She reached over for his hand and held it tightly. "I want you... but shit is just so complicated for me right now."

Now it was time for Bakari to remain silent. Indira moved closer to him to peck his lips a couple times before entwining their lips together in a deeper, passionate kiss. While their tongues danced, Indira placed her hands to his neck, bringing him closer to her. When she noticed how he refused to hold her, she broke their lips apart.

"Bakari..."

"I want you to leave him," Bakari instructed sternly. "I don't care about how complicated it is. Nothing's complicated about how I feel about you and how you feel about me. And I know how selfish I sound right now, but I don't really give a damn. I want you and only you. I've wanted you for years but always held back. However, now I'm not holding back for shit. I want you, and I intend to have you, Indira. Leave him."

Before she could respond, Bakari branded their lips back together.

Their passionate kiss continued, and before Indira knew it, Bakari had pulled her up from her seat onto his lap.

When she felt his hands start to pull on her sweatpants, fear overcame her, and she placed a hand on his chest to pull away from him.

"Bakari... we're not alone," she whispered shyly.

"I don't care," he said casually and continued to pull down her sweats. "You're riding this dick, right now."

Once he had managed to pull her sweats past her thighs, he looked behind her shoulder to see his driver focused on the road ahead.

"Sebastian, don't turn around for the next few minutes unless you want to die."

"Yes, sir."

"And don't look in the front view mirror, not once, or I promise you that's the last look you'll ever get," he warned him tensely. "And put on my playlist."

The tense tone that he was speaking in was one that Indira rarely heard from him. She could also see the deadly look in his eyes as he looked behind her. This man was a beast and was completely unapologetic about it. Then the deadly look vanished from his eyes when he stared back at her. Instead, a lustful gaze was now cradled in his pupils.

"You ready to ride this dick?" he seductively asked her.

"You're crazy, Kari," she whispered innocently.

"And you love it," he told her simply before raising her up slightly off his lap. Without even needing to be coached on what to do, Indira quickly pulled down his pants, followed by his boxers, and reached for his erect dick.

The seductive sounds of Marsha Ambrosius's "With You" sounded through the Bentley car's speakers as Indira's intoxicating ride began.

"Mmmh, shit," Indira quietly moaned, trying to keep her moans to a minimal level. She still couldn't believe that Bakari was giving it to her in the back seat while his driver drove.

Up and down, her body rocked on his dick, and his hold tightened on her ass cheeks. The quicker she bounced on his shaft, the better it felt.

"Shit," she cursed under her breath, deciding to muffle her moans in his neck. There may have been music playing in the background, but

Indira knew how loud she could get. The music wouldn't mask her moans completely.

"Di... aghhh, fuck," he groaned as her walls clenched around his hardness. "You gon' leave... him, right?"

"Mmh," her muffled moans sounded, beginning to heighten.

"Answer me," he demanded, squeezing her ass cheeks and using his hands to control her speed as she rode him. He took over and pushed her up and down according to his own choice. A choice that was only driving Indira crazier. "You gon' leave that nigga?"

"Bakari, ahh!" She released a loud whimper as he slid her wildly up and down. Her juices were coating the entire exterior of his shaft, and she could feel how wet her inner thighs were. "Pleaseee."

"No." He dismissed her pleads. "You're going to leave him and you... fuck! You're going to be with me."

"Uh-huh," she agreed with moans. The way he refused to slow down and pushed her tight slit down the entire length of his dick was only driving her insane.

"What was that?"

"Yes!" She agreed with the words he wanted to hear. "I'll leave... him."

"You promise?"

"Yes! Uhh, I promise, baby."

"I feel bad."

"Don't be, beautiful," Yasir voiced.

"I don't even wanna eat in front of you."

Yasir chuckled lightly. "I told you it's fine. Don't sweat about it."

"But you're fasting, Yasir, and here I am ea—"

He cut her off. "It's Ramadan, something I'm used to. Trust me, baby girl, it's cool. Besides, I'll break my fast at midnight, so don't worry about me. Just eat your food."

Arjana gave him a sympathetic look before following his words and eating her meal. They were currently on their lunch break for the day, and Yasir had decided to take Arjana out for lunch. The only problem was Arjana realized that Yasir wasn't ordering anything and then she remembered what month it was. May, which meant that it was Ramadan, and he was fasting. She felt bad and didn't want to tempt him by eating in front of him. However, Yasir insisted that it was okay.

"Yeah, eat up," he instructed with a smirk. "Because when I break my fast at midnight, best believe the first thing I'm gonna eat up is you."

Arjana's shyness could not be concealed as she looked at him and continued to eat her meal. Seeing as he had her undivided attention right now, Yasir saw this as the perfect time to bring up something that was heavy on his mind.

"Ana, I wanna talk to you about Jaden."

Arjana felt her heart skip a beat at the mention of Yasir's son.

Seeing as she hadn't said anything in response to him yet, he decided to keep talking.

"I know you've met him once before, but I really want you to meet him again and to keep on meeting him. With us now back together, I just wa—"

"We're back together?" Arjana dropped her fork and gave him a frosty look.

"Ana, stop playing. You know we are," he confirmed.

"I was not aware of this at all."

"Oh, so now you're back on your bullshit, huh?" he asked her tensely. "I'm not about to argue with you about this when we both know that you and I are in a relationship."

"Well I'm more than willing to argue with you, nigga. We're not tog—"

"Arjana!"

His yell had not only suddenly silenced her, but all the people also sitting in the restaurant that they were currently in. Arjana had glanced around to see that people were giving them strange looks.

"Yasir, you're causing a sc—"

"I really don't give a fuck!" he fumed with a pissed off facial expression. "You're really starting to piss me off because you know how in love with you I am. You know that I would die for you if I had to. I've done everything you've ever wanted. I've given you all of me. I know how rough life has been for you, and I've tried my hardest not to add any more turmoil to your life. I'm here to bring out the best in you. I've wanted to be your protector, provider, and most importantly, your man, from the second I laid eyes on you. Any problems, issues, or complications you've ever had since coming into my life, I've gladly took on as my own and helped you get through it. Even when you constantly push me away, I'm still always here for you. Even when you treat me like shit, I still stay right by your side like a fool.

You can't keep playing these silly little games and think it's gonna run, because I promise you that it won't. You think I'm going to stand aside and take this shit forever? Well I promise you, Ana, that I fuckin' won't. I love you, but I also love you enough to let you go. You don't want us to be together? Alright, cool, then no more playing these dumbass games. Stop calling me at 2 a.m. in the fuckin' morning, telling me how much you love me, need me and this dick. And I admit I'm not perfect. I admit me messing around with you at work is inappropriate, but when you're all I think about and all I want, how can I stay away from you? But it's cool. If staying away from you is what you want me to do, then I'll be more than willing to do so. Just know that you can't keep playing with us and think I'm going to wait for your ass to wake the fuck up and realize what's right in front of you."

After his speech, Yasir furiously got up from his seat, pulled out dollar bills onto the table, and stormed out from the restaurant, leaving Arjana by herself.

Chapter Sixteen

"Shit... princess, I'm... I'm close."

Tokyo gazed up at him with a smile in her eyes before she pushed her mouth all the way down to his base.

"God damn it, T... you nasty girl."

Giving men head was actually quite rare for Tokyo. She didn't just do it to anyone. It was something that she considered to be extremely intimate. Being willing to place her mouth on a man's private area meant that she really liked him, and when it came to Adonis, like was beginning to become an understatement.

Adonis was in pure bliss right now. Pure ecstasy. Watching and feeling her soft pink lips sucking on his dick was wonderful. Faster and faster, her head bobbed up and down his long length, making his erection grow stronger.

He even gently ran his fingers through her hair as her lips worked their magic. Her hands stayed situated at the base of his dick, twisting and turning while her tongue did the main work up top.

All it took was a few more minutes of her slurping, sucking, and choking on his shaft before his load came shooting into her mouth and down her throat.

"You little freak," he whispered to her with a grin once she had swallowed his cum and sucked his dick completely dry.

Tokyo only grinned back at him and licked her lips before getting up to sit on his lap.

"That's just my little way of saying thank you for bringing me lunch."

"Well if that's your way of saying thank you, then I need to start bringing you a full three-course meal."

Tokyo released a giggle and smiled at him happily. "A three-course meal sounds good."

"Good," he replied coolly, stroking her arm. "Because I'm cooking for you tonight."

All Tokyo could do was smile harder and feel complete awe for this man right in front her. What she had done to deserve him, she didn't know, but she was thankful that God had placed him in her life. He was so loving, so considerate, and so perfect. She knew it was early days, but she could honestly say that she was falling for Adonis. Her only hope was that things remained good between them.

An hour later, Adonis had left, which meant that Tokyo needed to get back to work. She checked on all her workers for about thirty minutes until she got a call from her iPhone. It had been an unexpected call, but nothing was more surprising than when she saw the caller ID.

"Kazimir? Girl! It's been forever!... Yeah, I'm good girl. How are you? How's Santorini been?... That's so good to hear... Oh you're back now?... Oh great! So I'll be seeing you real soon then... Oh sure. You want your hair and lashes done?... Of course, girl. You gotta look good for your man, I get it, I get it... Yeah, I got you. Just come 'round tomorrow at 1:30 p.m. for your appointments... Yeah, great!... Alright, love, take care, and I'll see you tomorrow."

Once getting off the phone, Tokyo immediately texted her sister. *Kaz's back!*

Arjana responded seconds later: *I know. She just texted me.*

Arjana: *I'm excited to see her.*

Tokyo: *Same, it's been ages.*

Arjana: *Mom's definitely gonna organize a family dinner to celebrate her return.*

Tokyo: *Without a doubt.*

Arjana: *You should invite new boy.*
Tokyo: *Nah... too soon.*
Arjana: *Says the girl who got choked with her own wig by him.*
Tokyo: *LMAO!*
Tokyo: *I'm lowkey still traumatized by that.*
Tokyo: *It was sexy as fuck to me though.*
Tokyo: *I think I love him for real.*
Arjana: *T, what the hell? Tell me you're joking?*
Tokyo: *Looooool!*
Tokyo: *I don't think I am.*
Tokyo: *He clapped my shit like a standing ovation.*
Tokyo: *I cried when he first ate me out.*
Tokyo: *I think I wanna buy him some shoes.*
Arjana: *Get outta here, T.*
Arjana: *Did you not just say it's too soon?*
Tokyo: *Yeah but... he's amazing.*
Arjana: *I pray he doesn't fuck up because only God knows what you'll do.*
Tokyo: *Oh he's a dead man walking 110%. So he better not mess up.*
Arjana: *You free tonight for drinks?*
Arjana: *I need to vent to you about Yasir.*
Tokyo: *Sorry sis... not tonight. I'll be too busy on my man's dick.*
Tokyo: *Tomorrow for sure.*
Arjana: *Alrightieee, ditch me for some dick as per usual.*
Tokyo: *It ain't even like that. I'm just letting my kitty live her best life since we've been a drought.*
Arjana: *Well the drought is most definitely over!*
Tokyo: *It definitely is!*
Arjana: *Tomorrow then sis.*
Tokyo: *Tomorrow x*

~ Later That Evening ~

Adonis looked down to see that Tokyo was fast asleep. After the wood he had given her, he was surprised that she wasn't in a coma already. He gently shifted his body away from hers, being extra careful not to wake her up before rolling out of bed.

He then picked up his phone and headed to the bathroom. As he took a leak, all he could think about was how beautiful Tokyo was. She was even more beautiful in person than he had seen in pictures. To make things even worse, she was a good kisser and even better in bed. That was just some of the reasons why this was becoming more difficult for Adonis. But he knew he had a job to do and was sticking to it regardless.

Zing! Zing! Zing!

Adonis stared down at his vibrating device by the sink only to see the notification for an incoming FaceTime video call. He quickly accepted the call and lifted the phone to his face.

"Baby?"

Her angelic, pretty face appeared on his bright screen, and hearing her soft voice made him crack a small smile.

"What's up, princess?"

"Don, I miss you, that's what's up." She turned with a pout. "When are you coming back home to me?"

"Xaveria, you know I'm handling business right now," he reminded her firmly. "Important business."

"Well hurry up and get it done," she responded bossily. "I miss my man."

"And he misses you too, princess," he informed her in a softer tone. "But daddy's got to deal with the bitch that killed Carl. Then I'll be back home before you know it."

Chapter Seventeen

Indira picked up her Givenchy tote side bag and placed it on her shoulder before heading out of her bedroom. It was only when she got into the corridor of the hallway leading into the living room that she saw the front door being pulled open. In Javon stepped with a neutral expression until he laid eyes on her.

Indira felt awkward as they stared at each other. Instead of either of them speaking up, Indira walked toward the door, not wanting to be late for work. However, as soon as she got to the door, Javon still stood in her way.

"I've got to get to work," she informed him stiffly.

"Indi," he gently called out to her. "Can we talk, please? It feels like I haven't talked to my fiancée for years. I specifically asked my brother to look after our dad this week so I could come home to talk to you."

Indira gave him a blank stare before responding, "Well talking right now doesn't seem like the smartest idea when I'm on my way to work."

"Okay," Javon agreed. "When you come back."

"Alright," she said with an exhale.

"But we really do need to talk, Indira. Something's changed between us, and I don't like it at all. We're engaged to be married in less than two months, but it doesn't feel like it anymore. It feels like you don't care about me no more. Like I'm not even your man anymore. You don't even wear your ring anymore, Indi. What's up with that?"

Indira swallowed hard as she looked up at him. His mention of their engagement and relationship in general made Indira think back to Bakari's demand of her breaking up with Javon for good. It had only been three days since their Cuba trip, but still his words remained heavy on her mind. She was slightly torn on what to do, because a part of her wanted to be with Bakari, but leaving Javon wasn't something that she was expecting to do.

Just over a month ago, she was certain that Javon was who she was going to spend the rest of her life with. The man that she was going to make loads of babies with. The man that she had history with. But even though they had history together, her and Bakari clearly had stronger chemistry together. She felt more comfortable with him and more able to be herself.

"You're right," she finally agreed with him. "We do need to talk."

The one thing that Indira knew had to be done was coming clean about her infidelities. Keeping this affair or whatever it was that she was doing with Bakari was something she was no longer willing to keep concealed from Javon. It was wrong for her to be stringing him along like this when she knew fully well that she had feelings for another man.

Once I tell him tonight, it's over between us. Even if he wants to forgive me, which he most likely won't do, it's time for us to part. I've made my decision. I want to be with Bakari only. He's been nothing but loyal to me and never given me a reason to not trust him. I'm the only woman he wants; he said so himself.

"Great. I'll be waiting," he said as he gave her a gentle smile. "Have a good day at work."

It was only a few minutes later that Indira had headed to work, leaving Javon alone at their home.

He had arrived from his father's home after spending the night there, and the one thing he wanted to do was shower then rest. So he headed to their bedroom and started undressing.

It was only when he was fully undressed with nothing but a towel wrapped around his waist that he heard the front door open and shut. Already knowing who had come through the door, Javon ignored it and entered the en-suite bathroom.

Javon stared at his reflection in the mirror, looking peacefully at himself. He slowly took his towel off his body, ready to have his shower.

Fifteen minutes later, Javon was finished with his hot, soothing shower and walked back into his bedroom, only to see her laying on the cotton sheets, completely naked for him.

He quickly dropped his towel to the ground and stepped out of it before climbing onto the bed and reaching for her legs.

She giggled excitedly when he aggressively pulled her down the bed, and when he flipped her over, she was more than ready for him.

"I missed you, Von... oooh."

"I know you did, Siobhan. This dick missed you even more. Do you want it?" he asked her seductively.

"You know I want it, baby... Give it to me now," she moaned, grinding on his tip slowly. He slowly began pounding into her, gripping tightly onto her waist with one hand and repeatedly spanking her ass hard with the other. "Yesss, just like that, Von. Fuck me. Faster!"

Twenty minutes later and the pair were completely exhausted. Javon gazed down to see the never-ending grin on her pink lips, and she gave him a curious stare as she held onto him tighter.

"What's wrong?"

Javon sighed deeply as he shut his eyes momentarily before opening them again.

"We can't keep doing this shit, Siobhan."

Siobhan decided to say nothing and break eye contact with him.

"We need to stop."

"I don't want to stop," she muttered. "We never stop."

"And that's exactly why," he began, lifting her chin up so he was forced to look at him. "We need to stop."

"It's too good for us to ever stop. You know this, Javon. So what's the point of trying? We'll just fail again."

"Well for starters, you need to stop moving in and out. You need your own official spot where you stay permanently. You're a grown ass woman, Siobhan. You can't keep depending on your daughter. You have more than enough money to stay in your place. With all the money I give you, you know damn well you're not broke."

"Neither are you, but you stay asking her for money. Didn't she buy you a car last month? You know damn well you could have bought that money with your own savings in the bank. And you know damn well you don't struggle to keep a job. Why you keep lying to her about getting fired is beyond me. You deserve an Oscar with the way you effortlessly fool her. Just come clean to her about you selling dope. Besides, I only keep moving in so I can be close to you, Von. So we can be close to you. I don't want to go."

"You need to. I can't have you and Noah here when I'm trying to get things between Indira and I back on track. We've drifted, but I intend to fix that," he explained seriously. "I'm not telling her about me selling dope because I don't intend to do that shit for long. Just a few more months then I'll get a regular job again."

"Why can't Noah and I be here?" she asked him incredulously. "He's your son too. He's needs to be close to his father."

Javon gave her a guilty look and stayed quiet.

Siobhan was an attractive woman. An extremely attractive woman. She always had been, so trying to resist her was something that Javon struggled with completely. But getting her pregnant the first time was shocking.

"Besides," Siobhan started to speak up, "I'm pregnant again, Javon. And I'm not aborting this one like you made me get rid of the last one before Noah. I want another baby with you."

I can't wait to hear you moan my name tonight.

Bakari.

Indira helplessly blushed at his text message before remembering that tonight she planned to confess to Javon her sins. So seeing Bakari was unlikely, but she didn't want to rule it out.

Before she could finish typing her response to him, the sound of two knocks sounded on her door.

Knock! Knock!

"Come in."

The door was pushed open to reveal the pretty face of her boss, and there was a figure behind her who she couldn't see the face of properly until she stepped in.

"Indi, this is the client I was talking about that I needed you to fit in," Tokyo announced with a graceful smile. "Kazimir, meet Indira, the best lash tech ever. Indira, meet Kazimir."

Indira laid eyes on Kazimir's face and was immediately taken aback due to her beauty. Stunning was an understatement for this woman right here. She was a milk chocolate goddess with skin so smooth and flawless looking that it made Indira feel insecure about her own skin. Her jet black, long hair went past her hips and seemed to stop at the middle of her ass. Her hair framed her oval head which housed her hypnotic sienna brown eyes, thin arched brows, full shapely pink lips, and her body? Her body was to die for. She was thick in all the right places; she had thick thighs which accentuated her curves, large breasts, and from the tight lace bodysuit she wore, Indira could clearly see her flat stomach.

"Nice to meet you," Indira spoke up. "You're beautiful by the way."

"Oh my gosh. Thank you so much," Kazimir responded. "You're so pretty too."

"I'll leave the two of you alone," Tokyo concluded, feeling satisfied that they were getting along.

Once Tokyo had left, Indira instructed Kazimir to take a seat on the white recliner and lay down so she could begin the lash appointment.

One thing that Indira's clients always said they loved about getting their lashes done with her was the fact that the appointments included a free therapy session. Because that's exactly what it felt like to them as they had deep, interesting conversations with her. They basically opened up to her on a personal level because she made them feel comfortable enough to do so. And that's exactly what was happening now with Kazimir as she got her eyelash extensions done.

"So where are you from?" Kazimir curiously asked.

"Born and raised in Atlanta, girl."

"Seriously? So you've been here your whole life?"

"Uh-huh," Indira confirmed as she placed a mink lash onto Kazimir's lash line. "What about you? Were you raised here?"

"No. I was raised in Michigan for a few years, but I'm originally from Haiti."

"Oh, so you're Haitian? That's cool. I know someone special from there..." Thoughts of Bakari filled Indira's head.

"Yeah, that's where I'm from."

"So what brings you to Atlanta?"

"I'm back in town to be with my fiancé," Kazimir said with a happy smile. "I was away on business, but I'm back now."

"Oh, that's great to hear. You guys must have missed each other so much. When's the wedding?"

"We haven't set a date yet, but now that I'm back in town, hopefully, in the next few months."

"Aww, that's good to hear," Indira commented.

"How long have you worked for Tokyo?" Kazimir queried.

"It's going eight months now."

"Oh, cool! Did you know her before?"

"Yeah, we were in high school together. I've known her for years."

"Oh my gosh? Really?" Kazimir questioned her, clearly full of surprise. "So you must know Bakari?"

Indira felt her heart skip a beat at the mention of him.

"Yeah, I do," she informed her calmly as she gently combed out her lashes. "How do you know him?"

"Girl, that's my sexy ass fiancé," Kazimir proudly announced.

Indira almost dropped the lash comb she was holding in her hands which would have resulted in the comb dropping on Kazimir's eye.

"S-Sorry?" Indira thought that maybe she had misheard her, but she hadn't.

"Bakari is my fiancé. We've been engaged for almost a year now. Here's the ring he bought me."

Indira observed with a bated breath as Kazimir lifted up her left hand, and the large diamond rock on her finger almost blinded her. "We're planning to spend the rest of our lives together, forever."

To Be Continued...

A Note From Author

Uh-oh... Back again with a brand-new series! I hope you guys enjoyed reading about Bakari, Indira, and the rest of the new gang. The drama has just begun, and I promise that it's only going to get crazier. This is going to be a *crazy* ride. I hope you're ready!

Please head over to my official website where you'll be able to see the visuals of Indira and Bakari, including the rest of the gang: www.missjenesequa.com. My website also includes **ALL** the visuals from my previous works, so don't hesitate to go check it out! And make sure you join my readers group on Facebook to stay in touch with me and my upcoming releases: www.facebook.com/groups/miss-jensreaders. I'll be posting sneak peeks from the next part in my readers group, so make sure you're a part of it!

Thank you so much for reading! I appreciate and love you guys soooo much. I'm always thanking God for bringing you wonderful readers into my life. Thank you for supporting me and motivating me to deliver some new books to you all.

Love From,
#TheFreakInTheBooks.

Miss Jenesequa

Miss Jenesequa
#TheFreakInTheBooks

Full Catalog

About The Author

Miss Jenesequa is a best-selling African American Romance & Urban Fiction novelist. Her best-known works are 'Bad For My Thug', which debuted at #1 on the Amazon Women's Fiction Bestseller list, 'Loving My Miami Boss', 'He's A Savage But He Loves Me Like No Other' and 'Sex Ain't Better Than Love' which have all debuted top 5 on Amazon Bestseller lists.

Born and raised in London, UK where she always dreamed of becoming successful at anything she put her mind to. In 2013, she began writing full length novels and decided to publish some of her work online through Wattpad. The more she continued to notice how much people were enjoying her work, the more she continued to deliver. Royalty via Wattpad found Jenesequa and brought her on as a published author in 2015. Her novels are known for their powerful, convincing storylines and of course filled with drama, sex and passion. And they are definitely not for the faint-hearted. If you're eager and excited to read stories that are unique to any you've read before, then she's your woman.

Stay Connected

Miss Jenesequa's Reading Room

Feel free to connect personally with Miss Jenesequa at:
www.missjenesequa.com

Thank you so much for reading! Don't forget to leave a review on Amazon. I'd love to know what you thought about my novel. ♥

f facebook.com/missjensworld

instagram.com/missjenesequa_

Royalty Publishing House is now accepting manuscripts from aspiring or experienced urban romance authors!

WHAT MAY PLACE YOU ABOVE THE REST:

Heroes who are the ultimate book bae: strong-willed, maybe a little rough around the edges but willing to risk it all for the woman he loves.

Heroines who are the ultimate match: the girl next door type, not perfect - has her faults but is still a decent person. One who is willing to risk it all for the man she loves.

The rest is up to you! Just be creative, think out of the box, keep it sexy and intriguing!

If you'd like to join the Royal family, send us the first 15K words (60 pages) of your completed manuscript to submissions@royaltypublishinghouse.com

LIKE OUR PAGE!

Be sure to LIKE our Royalty Publishing House page on Facebook!